The Dark City

THE
LAST APPRENTICE

The Dark City

IMOGEN ROSSI

HOT
KEY
BOOKS

With special thanks to Rosie Best

First published in Great Britain in 2014 by Hot Key Books
Northburgh House, 10 Northburgh Street, London EC1V 0AT

A CIP catalogue record for this book is available from the British Library.

ISBN: 978-1-4714-0250-0

1

This book is typeset in 11pt Sabon using Atomik ePublisher
Printed and bound by Clays Ltd, St Ives Plc

FSC

Hot Key Books supports the Forest Stewardship Council (FSC),
the leading international forest certification organisation, and is
committed to printing only on Greenpeace-approved FSC-certified paper.
www.hotkeybooks.com

Hot Key Books is part of the Bonnier Publishing Group
www.bonnierpublishing.com

For Poppy, Edie and Bethany

Chapter One

I'm racing along the dim passageways, gasping with laughter. It's like I'm flying, my feet barely touching the floor. I'm running so fast that the glowing starscape of paint specks on the stone walls blurs into a sparkling rainbow in the corner of my eye.

I don't think I've been this happy in a long time – not since the death of Master di Lombardi. But now the traitors who killed him are gone I can spend my days painting, and racing my friends through the world that di Lombardi created.

We're coming to the last corner . . . and I'm definitely going to win this time!

But another peal of laughter rings out right behind me. *No!* 'Not this time, Your Highness!' I yell.

I clench my fists and put on a burst of speed, but it's no good. Just as I round the bend, Duchess Catriona passes me in a rustle of silk, her red hair streaming out behind her like a banner.

'Bad luck, Bianca!' Catriona cackles. I push on, ignoring the Duchess's taunts. I can see the white door that marks the finish line – just a few more steps and I'll be back in the lead.

Then the door beside the white one bangs open and Marco tumbles into the passage, his dark curls dripping with sweat. He leaps across the passage and slams his hand on to the white door.

'I win!' he gasps. The Duchess and I both stagger to a halt, leaning on our knees to catch our breath. 'I had to . . . jump across from the palace roof, and climb down the tower of San Fernando's, and run through the monks' herb garden, but I beat you!'

'Being an acrobat is cheating,' the Duchess says. She grins and pats Marco on the back. 'No normal person could beat us from my drawing room to here without using the secret passages!'

'Not my fault I'm so talented,' Marco says. He pulls the paintbrush key from his pocket and presents it to me with a flourish. 'Mistress.'

My stomach twists uneasily as I accept the brush and turn it over in my hand, running my finger over the thin copper key and then over the soft hairs of the paintbrush on its other end. 'Don't, Marco,' I say, as we walk away from the white door. 'Don't treat me like a courtier, I am –'

I step around a corner, and my throat closes over the words.

Two figures stand just ahead of me, their faces and bodies swathed in sweeping dark cloaks. One carries a lantern, and as he raises it to check the symbol on one of the doors, the light falls on his features.

The round, red face of the Baron da Russo.

I seize Marco and the Duchess's sleeves and drag them back before the Baron can see them. I press myself to the wall and peer around the corner, trying not to breathe.

'Hurry!' The whisper is unmistakably real, horrifyingly close. 'We must get through!'

I know that voice. A chill lifts the hairs on the back of my neck. A glance at my friends tells me that they've recognised it too – Marco's face is pale, and Catriona's a furious red.

The voice belongs to Piero Filpepi, the artist who helped the Baron poison Master di Lombardi. They attempted to kill the Duchess too.

'Traitors!' Catriona hisses.

'It can't be,' whispers Marco. 'They vanished into that dark world – how can they be back?'

'This is the one,' the Baron says. I watch as the door swings open. It's painted black, the panels edged in a blue so bright they seem to glow.

Strange . . . I've never seen that door before.

The two men step through the door, and I clench my fists. They aren't going to get away from me, not again!

Duchess Catriona puts a restraining hand on my shoulder. 'I won't let you endanger yourself,' she snaps. 'Marco, run and fetch Captain Raphaeli and the palace guards.'

'There's no time!' The traitors are gone and the door is swinging shut. I shrug off the Duchess's hand and sprint along the corridor, reaching out to grab the door, and leap through.

Darkness envelops me, but I breathe in cool, fresh air. It only takes a second for my eyes to adjust, and then I can make out the lines of buildings rising all around me. The Baron and Filpepi are disappearing through a stone archway ahead. I start after them, vaguely aware of the door closing behind me.

On the other side of the archway I stop, taking in the strange beauty of the place I find myself standing in.

It's the dark city! This is the place I caught just a glimpse of as the two traitors made their escape.

Their hooded figures hurry away down a wide avenue beside the glittering black waters of a canal. There are no bright stars or moon to light the streets as they would do in La Luminosa. Coloured beams of light spill from the doorways and windows of the houses by the canal. Instead of the blazing lanterns that line the streets of La Luminosa at night, blue and green bolts of lightning crackle in thunder-lamp orbs on top of tall black iron poles.

I keep close to the shadow of the houses and follow Filpepi and the Baron. They scuttle through the darkness, across a bridge and down a small alley which comes out into a crowded market square. Merchants and their customers stroll from stall to stall. It's a lot like the Piazza del Fiero in La Luminosa – I can see stalls selling dangling black sausages and huge flat brown mushrooms, piles of books with dark leather covers embossed with silver writing, gleaming iron tools for cooking or building . . .

'Fine silk, get your fine silk here, only two silver pieces a yard!' a lady's voice cries, and I turn to look at a stall laden with huge rolls of cloth. All of it black. 'Good quality wools and cottons! Ribbons and threads in every shade!' the stallholder says, pulling away a sheet to unveil a rainbow of brightly coloured ribbons that stand out like flames against the dark cloth.

She's just setting up her stall. Does that mean it's morning here?

I realise that the people here are all dressed like the citizens of La Luminosa, except that almost every piece of clothing is dark – at first I think they're all in black, but as I watch the customers crowd around the fabric stall I start to make out deep reds, blues, browns and greens.

A lady in a deep midnight-blue dress turns and stares at me. She taps the shoulder of the woman beside her, who wears a sea-green feather in her velvet cap, and nods towards me. I freeze, my heart in my mouth – I've let myself get distracted. Where are the Baron and Filpepi? Are these people all in league with the traitors?

But then I realise that my plain, cream-coloured linen dress stands out in this place. Just as someone wearing full funeral black would in the Piazza del Fiero.

I ignore the women and hurry to the other side of the square, but there's no sign of the men. Craning my neck to see over the crowd, I search for the two hooded figures, but they've vanished.

I feel a twinge of guilt . . . but as I gaze back at the market square, a different feeling floods over me. The traitors have escaped, and I'm lost in this unfamiliar city – but I don't feel lost. I'm not worried. I want to stay here.

I feel right at home.

Bianca blinked awake as the piercingly bright rays of a La Luminosa sunrise fell over her face. Shielding her eyes with one hand, she sat up in bed, curling her feet under her, and sighed.

7

Another dream about the dark city.

She ran her hands over the silky covers of her bed, still not quite used to the comfort of her new room in the Duchess's palace. The bed was an enormous four-poster, with feather pillows and clean cotton sheets – nothing like her small bed at the very top of Master di Lombardi's tall, cramped old house.

Slipping out of bed, she slid her feet into her soft, fur-lined slippers. She crossed the room, put out the night lamp, and went over to the window.

As the newest in a long line of Royal-Artists-In-Residence, Bianca had been given one of the best chambers in the palace. It was on the east side, where it caught the morning sun, and gave her a perfect view over the palace walls, across the sparkling waters of the Grand Canal, and down into the city itself.

She closed her eyes, feeling the warmth of the sunrise on her face. But the dream didn't melt away, like other dreams did – she could recall every stone of the dark city, every flash of bright colour, as if she'd really been there.

Opening her eyes, she leaned her forehead against the cool glass of the window, torn between two completely contradictory desires: she desperately wished her dreams were real, so that she could go back to that wonderful place, but the idea of the Baron or Filpepi finding their way to di Lombardi's secret passages again sent a shiver down Bianca's spine.

What if they really did come back?

Perhaps her sleeping mind was trying to work out what

she would do if the traitors returned. If so, it wasn't doing a great job. She always lost them right before she woke up.

It was a childish dream, a flaring of her wild imagination, and nothing more.

If only she could shake off her longing to stay in the dark city.

Chapter Two

Bianca pinched the bridge of her nose, trying not to let her frustration show.

'Please, Your Highness, if you would go back to your sketches –'

'Oh, Bianca, don't fuss!' said Duchess Catriona, rising from the low couch. She crossed the room and picked up a crystal jug filled with orange juice. 'I'm only getting something to drink.'

Bianca took a deep calming breath. It wouldn't do to raise her voice at a Duchess, even if Catriona was only two years older – and her friend. 'I'm sure one of the servants would be more than happy to bring you a drink, so you don't have to leave your work . . .'

'Nonsense. Helena's got plenty to do without me calling her in here. Lady's maids don't just sit around waiting for me to give them orders, you know, they have other tasks.'

Well, at least someone in this palace is getting something done! Bianca thought as Catriona poured out a glass of juice, drank it and poured another. She turned as if she was about to go back to her seat, then wandered over to the window instead.

Only a few weeks ago, Bianca had been sitting in this same room watching Master di Lombardi giving the Duchess her art lessons. She'd found it funny and endearing when Catriona fidgeted or argued or played pranks on her teacher.

It was very different now that *she* was the teacher.

How did Master di Lombardi manage to teach her anything? Bianca wondered. 'Please come back to your seat, My Lady,' she pleaded. 'I was explaining about the muscles in the leg . . .'

'What's the rush? Marco can hold that pose for days, can't you, Marco?'

'Mm-hmm,' said Marco. He was standing on a table in front of the Duchess's couch, balanced on one leg with the other curved up behind him and both arms out, as if he was walking a tightrope. Last week, after Bianca had spent an hour rearranging the walled garden outside the windows so that she would have new scenes to sketch, the Duchess had called them 'stupid old chairs and ferns and things' and insisted that she wouldn't have another lesson until she could draw some people. So Bianca had found people to draw – Marco – but the Duchess's concentration hadn't improved.

Duchess Catriona finally returned to her couch and Bianca walked around behind her to look at her sketch. It was still just a stick figure in messy charcoal. The Duchess had given its circular head a crude smiley face.

'All right,' said Bianca. 'As I was saying. The muscles in the leg –'

'Honestly Bianca, do I really need to know?' Duchess

Catriona complained, flicking her charcoal up in the air and catching it. 'I'm here for a lesson in art, not medicine!'

Oh, so you do know why you're here. Bianca squashed the thought before it could make it to her lips. 'My Lady, your figures will be flat and dull if you don't understand something of how the body works.' She pointed over to a gold-framed painting on the other side of the Duchess's chamber; it depicted riders resting by a stream in the rolling hills south of the city. The enchanted horses and riders moved as if alive – one figure dismounted from his horse as the great animal bent to take a drink from the sparkling pool. 'Look at that rider – see the way he pants, out of breath from the ride? You could never paint such a *respirare* if you didn't know how people's muscles move when they breathe.'

Catriona barely glanced at the painting, instead eyeing her own subject before her. 'Well, then, let's have a closer look, shall we?' said the Duchess, leaping to her feet again.

Bianca was wary of this sudden enthusiasm, but said, 'Yes, I suppose that can't hurt. See here.' Bianca pointed to the back and then the front of the leg that Marco was holding up in the air. 'These muscles are pulling tight, but these are more relaxed. That's what controls the position of the leg.'

'Yes, I see,' said Catriona. Bianca met her eyes and saw the flash of mischief in them. 'And what happens if I do *this*?' The Duchess whipped out her charcoal pencil and ran it along the bottom of Marco's foot, tickling him. He let out a spluttering laugh and his knee buckled. He crashed down on the table, catching himself on his hands at the last minute and tumbling onto the floor.

'Marco! Are you all right?' Bianca gasped, rushing over to him.

Marco rubbed his knee. 'Fine!' he said, through a brittle grin. 'Very funny, Duchess,' he said.

Bianca shook her head. 'Well, I don't think it was funny.' She stood and turned to face the Duchess. 'Duchess Catriona, that was a very mean thing to do, and I . . .' Catriona was staring down her nose at Bianca now, with that imperious look that meant she wanted whoever was speaking to stop *at once*. But Bianca folded her arms across her bodice and pressed on. 'There's no point in me giving you lessons if you don't even try. Art is hard, Your Highness, but it's important – at least to me.'

'It's important to me too!' Duchess Catriona said. 'I love my art lessons! You just need to relax, Bianca. Art should be fun!' She turned to Marco. 'I'm sorry if I hurt you, Marco. But come on, Bianca, you can be Artist-in-Residence and my friend at the same time, can't you?'

'Of course,' said Bianca. 'It's just that this residency is such an honour – I don't want to let you down. If I'm going to teach you then I'm going to make you the best artist I can.'

'And you are! Look, I'm sitting down, see?' Catriona sat in front of her sketching paper and grinned up at Bianca. 'Teach me. Go on. I promise I'll try to pay attention.'

Bianca grinned in relief. But before she could suggest Marco take up another, safer pose, the curtain over the door was pushed aside and a gaunt-faced old man in a blue velvet robe stepped into the room. Secretary Franco.

'My Lady, I apologise most sincerely for interrupting,' he

said. Bianca noted that he didn't ask if he should go away again. He crossed the room and bowed low in front of the Duchess, holding a large bundle of papers under one arm. 'I have urgent business from Your Highness's captains, and the evening tide will not wait for . . . *art*.' His lip curled a little, as if just saying the word 'art' left a foul taste in his mouth. 'If I may borrow you from your *lessons* for just a few minutes . . .' He cast Bianca and Marco a withering glance.

I suppose he's wondering what an apprentice and an acrobat can teach a Duchess, Bianca thought. She glanced at Catriona's sketch again and sighed. *And I don't blame him.*

The Duchess stood and swept Secretary Franco a mocking bow. 'At your service, My Lord. Let's get on with it.'

Secretary Franco laid out his bundle of papers on the table and produced quills, sealing wax and string from the pockets of his robe. Bianca and Marco stood respectfully aside, Marco still rubbing his knee, while Duchess Catriona signed her name ten or twelve times and Secretary Franco lit the wick on the sealing wax. Then Catriona picked up her seal, with the letter C and the blazing sun symbol of La Luminosa engraved on its metal end, and slammed it down into the soft wax on each document. She barely missed the old man's fingers.

'Is this all?' Catriona asked. 'You just needed me to sign these papers? If it's so urgent, couldn't I have done them yesterday, rather than in the middle of my art lesson?'

Secretary Franco gathered up the papers and cast another withering glance at Bianca and Marco. He leaned forward in a bow, and lowered his voice – though not enough that

Bianca couldn't hear every word. 'Your Highness may do as Your Highness pleases, of course, but . . . is Your Highness sure that drawing pictures is a good use of Your Highness's very precious time?'

'My Highness is completely sure of it!' Catriona barked, loud enough that the old man recoiled. 'Now go away!'

Secretary Franco bowed out of the room without another word.

Bianca took a deep breath. 'All right,' she said brightly. 'Why don't we try it with Marco sitting on the edge of the table? Duchess, let's –'

'How rude!' Duchess Catriona muttered, still glaring at the doorway. 'Franco, I mean. How dare he interrupt?'

Bianca sighed. 'Well, he obviously doesn't think he's interrupting anything important, Your Highness.'

The Duchess folded her arms over her bodice and went ominously still. Then she turned around, and Bianca realised they were never going to get back to the lesson. That mischievous light glinted in Catriona's eyes, just like it had before she'd tickled Marco's foot.

'I think Franco deserves to be taught a little lesson, don't you?'

I think he was just trying to do his job, thought Bianca. *Even if he was being rude about it.* She didn't really want to hesitate – she wanted to grin back at Catriona just like Marco was doing. Maybe the Duchess was right, maybe she was letting her new post get to her and she just needed to relax.

'How about after your lesson . . .' she began.

'No. After my lesson it'll be time for lunch, and then he always spends the afternoon with the scribes. We've got to get to him while he's in his study. You've got the key with you, right?'

'Well, yes, always, but – but you did bring me here to work, Your Highness, and you have to . . .'

'. . . *do the work you were set to do.*' Duchess Catriona spoke along with Bianca, finishing her sentence.

Bianca let out a giggle, recognising one of di Lombardi's well-worn sayings. Was she turning into her dour old master? As much as she had loved him, she didn't want to *be* him. 'Oh my stars. I really am getting old!' She grinned cheekily and whipped Master di Lombardi's magical paintbrush key from her pocket. 'Come on, let's do it! Let's have a bit of fun with that old grouch.'

They hurried over to the magical painting in the alcove beside a potted orange tree. It was a scene of a balcony overlooking a beautiful leafy landscape, enchanted so that it looked like a real extension of the room that you could walk into. The sun in the painted sky glowed and the leaves of the trees waved slightly in a magical breeze. Bianca smiled as she remembered Catriona hiding Master di Lombardi's special blue chalk underneath the painted couch inside the picture. That *had* been pretty funny. She hoped that secretly di Lombardi had thought so too.

Holding up the paintbrush, Bianca whispered, 'Hidden rooms, secret passages, second city!' The minuscule cogs inside the thin wooden handle of the paintbrush clicked and whirred as the handle slid away and the copper prongs folded out into the shape of a key. With another grin at the Duchess and Marco, Bianca stepped over the threshold into the painting and turned the key in the lock of the small wooden door at one side of the balcony. It swung open and she stepped through into the secret passages.

Bianca smiled as she breathed in the cool, fragrant air and ran her hand over a wall that looked and felt like stone but smelled like canvas and paint. This whole place had been painted into existence, a way to travel between every one of the magical paintings in La Luminosa. She guessed it had been di Lombardi who'd created the passages – but she still had no idea how, why or when it had been done.

'Lead the way, Bianca!' Catriona said, coming after her with Marco on her heels.

Bianca turned left from the Duchess's drawing room, then took the next right, and counted ten doors along as Marco and Catriona hurried behind her, laughing. She'd started to learn her way around, at least when it came to the most useful paintings inside the palace. The trick was to try and put the real world out of your head completely – paintings that were next door to each other in the secret passages might be miles apart in the real city. And there were still areas of the painted world she hadn't explored.

The painting in Secretary Franco's office was a sombre depiction of San Pietro studying the Elder Mysteries, surrounded by teetering piles of books, glimmering scientific instruments and a large, bleached white skull. The saint moved a little, not too much, just enough to give the impression that he was reading the page in front of him with great attention and wisdom.

Bianca opened the door at the back of the painting a tiny crack and Catriona and Marco crowded up behind her to see through into the office. Looking past the saint's elbow, Bianca could see Secretary Franco in almost the exact same pose, poring over a huge pile of parchments and scrolls. His beaky nose practically grazed the surface of the document on the top of the pile. The letters that Duchess Catriona had signed and sealed sat in a neat basket by his left hand.

'What should we do?' Marco whispered.

'I bet I could hit the back of his head from here, but I don't have anything to throw,' Duchess Catriona said thoughtfully, patting her pockets. 'Apart from my rings.'

'No.' Bianca pushed the door shut. 'Even if he didn't see us, where would he think it came from? I've got a better idea, let's just ruffle his feathers. I need something long and pointy.'

'I've got just the thing.' Duchess Catriona bent down, her huge, silky skirts pooling around her. Bianca winced as she grabbed the hem and ripped along the seam. 'It's all right, it's always getting caught on the roses when I go walking in the garden – Helena will just think it's torn itself on a bush.' She fiddled for a second and brought out a long, curved strip of thick wire.

Bianca took the wire with a grin. 'This is perfect!' She pulled it straight and reopened the door. Secretary Franco was still reading the same document – if anything he was moving even less than the painted saint.

Slowly, Bianca poked the stiff wire into the room until

it was right behind the secretary's back. As he reached for a pen on his right, Bianca jabbed to the left, toppling the basket of sealed documents onto the floor. Secretary Franco jumped several inches into the air, his velvet robe rippling around him. Bianca tugged the wire back quickly. Behind her, she heard the muffled sound of Duchess Catriona giggling through a mouthful of her own sleeve.

Secretary Franco sighed and bent down to his left to pick up the basket – so Bianca poked the stack of papers to his right. They flew up in the air like a flock of birds leaping from the branch of a tree. With a gasp, the secretary stood up and stared at the scattered papers, his mouth hanging open.

'Let me, let me!' whispered Marco. Bianca sniggered and pressed her finger to her lips. Marco took the wire and Bianca strained to see over his shoulder as he waited patiently for Secretary Franco to place the basket of trade agreements back on his desk and walk around to pick up the mess on the other side.

Marco hooked the big document that the Secretary had been studying and flipped it into the air, yanking the wire back at once. Secretary Franco spun around in time to gape in horror as the document floated back down to the desk.

'What in the name of the Duchess is going on?' he whispered to himself, standing by his desk as if ready to grab any other documents that decided to make a break for freedom, and Bianca saw Duchess Catriona sink to her knees in a puddle of silk skirts, her shoulders shaking with suppressed laughter.

Bianca looked back into the study just in time to catch

the large, elaborately written title of the big document as Secretary Franco seized it.

She gasped aloud, and then clamped her hands over her mouth. She felt as if she'd been slapped.

Franco didn't seem to have heard her gasp. He was muttering as he scribbled on a piece of paper. 'To whom it may concern . . . a summons . . . the reading of the will . . . reckoning of properties . . . final wishes . . . tomorrow, the twelfth of May, in the presence of Duchess Catriona, Her Royal Highness, Supreme Ruler of, etc, etc.' He signed the note with a flourish and folded it into an envelope.

Bianca slowly closed the door, and turned to Duchess Catriona and Marco. 'It's being read tomorrow.'

'What is?' asked Marco.

'My master's will,' she said.

Chapter Three

'I'm sorry, Bianca. I didn't know,' Duchess Catriona said, as they walked back through the passages. 'I haven't been through my appointments for tomorrow yet.'

Bianca let out a long breath. In all of the chaos and intrigue and adventure that'd followed di Lombardi's death, she'd forgotten that he would have written a will.

'I expect he's left everything to the Museum,' she said. 'He always said he was a servant of the Crown and the people, not just some private craftsman.'

Duchess Catriona took Bianca's hand and squeezed it tightly. 'He was a great man, Bianca. I still miss him every day.'

'Me too.' Bianca put her other hand into her pocket and ran the soft bristles of the paintbrush key over her palm, remembering her master.

Her sadness had softened over the last few weeks. At first it had come in horrible waves, sharp and unpredictable, as if every tenth tile in the palace had been loosened and was waiting to trip her up. Now it was more like a limp from an old wound – it was just *there*.

They found an empty room and clambered out through a painting of two young ladies warming up for a dancing lesson.

'I have to go. I've got a meeting with Ambassador Inchuk and I'm already late,' the Duchess said. Then she hugged Bianca fiercely. 'I'll see you tomorrow.'

Bianca nodded and she and Marco waved as the Duchess hurried off, the bottom of her dress trailing without its wire.

'Good morning, Miss Bianca,' said a voice, and Bianca turned to see a maid bobbing a curtsey as she scurried past.

'Good – oh,' Bianca began, but the maid was gone. 'I don't know if I'm ever going to get used to that,' she said to Marco, shaking her head as they started back to the Duchess's drawing room. 'They don't wait for me to answer, they just curtsey whenever they see me and run off. It's weird!'

'You're special now,' Marco smirked. He swept a low bow and seized her hand like a fancy gentleman from one of his father's plays. 'A master artist!'

'Geroff,' Bianca laughed. 'I'm not special. And I'm *definitely* not a master.' She wasn't nearly a good enough artist to be called *master*.

Marco shrugged. 'You're going to have to get used to people treating you all poshly if you live in the palace,' he said.

'Why? *You* live in the palace, and you spend almost as much time with the Duchess as I do and nobody pretends you're a gentleman!'

'Charming,' said Marco, but he grinned. 'Tumblers aren't

respectable, not like artists.'

They turned a corner into the Rose Gallery and Bianca's heart skipped a beat. It was here, while she was working on the huge mural that took up the length of the corridor, that she'd discovered the secret of the passages. She turned her face to the mural as they passed, feeling the warmth and light from the painted greenhouse on her face. Inside the bright glass structure, raised earth beds lined the ochre-tiled floor and Bianca couldn't help trailing her arm into the magical painting, grazing the delicate petals of the rose bushes, their scent flooding her nostrils. At the end of the flowerbed was a door – seemingly leading to a painted building. But it was a door that led into the picture and to a secret passage – the first she'd ever painted. She remembered the joy that'd surged through her when she'd realised she could create a real door out of magical paint.

She was distracted from her reverie when a woman dressed as a mermaid marched through the door in front of them and stopped dead. She plonked her hands on her hips, ruffling her blue-green scaly tights, and tossed the twisted fabric strands of her blue wig over her shoulder.

'Marco!' the mermaid snapped. 'There you are! We've been looking for you everywhere!'

'Oh sorry, Olivia,' Marco said. 'I got, um . . . waylaid.'

'Well, come on,' Olivia snapped. 'We've got a scene to rehearse and this wig is itching like mad.'

Marco just about managed a wave and a 'see you later' to Bianca before Olivia herded him out of the gallery, still muttering about the wig.

'Bye.' Bianca sighed to herself. She wondered what Rosa and Cosimo and her old master's other apprentices were doing right now. *They* would certainly never curtsey to her.

She turned around and almost walked into a tall man in a cream velvet doublet trimmed with white fur. 'Oh sorry, My Lord.'

The man gave her a wide, slick smile. 'Ah, dear little Bianca,' he said, bowing almost as low as Marco had. Bianca curtseyed back and tried to remember that it was wrong to give dirty looks to lords – even if they did call you 'dear little Bianca'.

'Lord di Cassio,' she said, and tried to step aside.

'Actually, Bianca, I was looking for you!' di Cassio said. He gave her another oily grin. 'I wanted to talk to you; I know you were just giving our beloved Duchess her art lesson, and I was wondering if she said anything about the matter of Lady Rosalita's dowry.'

Bianca rolled her eyes. If it wasn't cringing servants, it was courtiers like di Cassio – they all had something they wanted her to talk to the Duchess about. People like him wouldn't have given her a second glance two weeks ago, unless it was to tell her to get out of their way.

'Um, not right now, I'm very busy – Artist-In-Residence business,' she said, neatly sidestepping the courtier and making a break for the Duchess's private drawing room.

She made it, but she still wasn't alone. The Duchess's drawing room was full of maids. They were sweeping the floor, plumping up the cushions on the couch, taking away the juice and making it seem as if the room cleaned itself by magic every time the Duchess left. They all dropped what they were doing and bobbed curtseys to Bianca, and then stood still with their eyes averted so they wouldn't meet her gaze.

Guilt burned the back of Bianca's throat and she hurried to clear away the Duchess's art things. None of the maids would be able to get on with their jobs until she was gone. She rolled the coloured chalks into their case, folded up the easel, scooped up the rather small pile of sketches, and shoved all of them into her canvas bag.

She hurried out, clutching the bag tight. She had to find somewhere she could be alone, without servants or lords or ambassadors or actors watching her every move. If she was going to get anything done as Duchess Catriona's Artist-In-Residence, she had to get some peace and quiet!

For the first time since she'd spotted Master di Lombardi's will, Bianca felt a warm smile spread across her face. *I know just the place.*

The old Duke's sitting room. It had been shut ever since the Duke's death.

Bianca stepped into the sitting room and looked up at the breathtaking scene of life and movement in the exotic garden painted on the wall. Two majestic tigers lay curled together in the foreground, under the dappled shade of a glossy green fern. A lion stalked back and forth between two trees, sometimes stopping to wash its forepaws just like the cats that hung around the palace kitchens.

Bianca walked through the thick dust on the floor and stepped into the garden. She reached out as she passed the lion and ran her hand through its bright yellow mane. It parted just like real fur, but if she shut her eyes the strands felt more like the frayed ends from a piece of canvas that had unravelled.

The lion was so lifelike, with its huge pink tongue rasping over the back of its paws, that she almost expected it to look up and rub its head against her side. But of course, it was only a picture that'd been given the illusion of life. It went on doing the sequence of actions it'd been enchanted to do.

Bianca glanced back at the wonderful garden before she stepped through the old wooden door at the back of the painting and into the secret passages. She found herself directly opposite the short corridor leading to Master di Lombardi's secret workshop.

It was wonderfully good luck that the closest door to di Lombardi's workshop led into a room that nobody went into.

But is it luck? Bianca wondered, as she turned the key in the workshop door. Master di Lombardi had been the Duchess's spy and protector as well as a master artist. Knowing he foiled an assassination plot, Bianca could easily believe that he'd somehow arranged for the Duke's sitting room to stay shut up for years. There really was no limit to her old master's ingenuity.

Bianca stood and gazed around the workshop. Its hugeness still surprised her. There were separate, neatly laid-out benches for woodwork, metalwork, stonework, varnishing, soldering, sanding and more. In between the benches, di Lombardi's inventions hung on wires from the glass ceiling or sat on blocks like carts having their wheels replaced. She walked up to one of the contraptions and tried to follow its logic by running her fingers over its odd combination of pipes and shovels and glass tubes. She still hadn't worked it out.

A metallic chirping high above made her look up. The mechanical bird that she'd found the first time she and Marco had discovered the workshop was fluttering between the hanging inventions. It swooped down and perched on one wing of the flying machine, tilting its head with a little clicking noise.

Bianca sighed as she looked at the flying machine, with its glorious mechanism of gas, steam, copper and huge expanses of leather. Its body was precariously balanced on top of one of the woodworking benches and one of the wings was propped against the wall, the other trailing on the floor. Taking off had been quite easy – especially when the Duchess's life had been in danger – but landing had been a lot harder. Now one of the pipes had burst and several cogs were bent.

She'd resolved to try and fix it as soon as she could spare the time . . . but so far something had always got in the way.

Cracking her knuckles, she headed for the soldering bench. As she pumped the bellows and ignited the thin gas flame that would heat up the iron, she thought about that crinkled piece of paper in the Secretary's hands – the Last Will and Testament of Annunzio di Lombardi.

Tears prickled at the corners of her eyes and Bianca wiped them away. She knew he was dead. That the one person who'd always given her his time and respect and – and yes, friendship, in his own way – was dead and buried in the cemetery of Santa Angelica.

But she still felt like he might come back to fix his flying machine.

They don't read wills for people who are coming back.

She shook herself, pulled on the thick heatproof gloves and seized the red-hot soldering iron and a length of copper wire.

That means it's up to me.

Bianca puffed and fumbled with the last few laces on the sleeves of her dress as she jogged along the corridor to the small dining room where her breakfast was laid out. She'd overslept, exhausted after a long afternoon and evening trying to fix the flying machine. She couldn't wait to tell Marco about her progress – it wasn't quite ready for another flight, but she'd found out how it worked: something to do with the air pressure in the steam chambers.

She burst into the dining room, expecting to see the tables crowded and buzzing with conversation and the tinkle and clank of plates and cutlery. But instead, they were barely half full, and the atmosphere seemed oddly subdued.

Bianca frowned. She was late, but not so late that she'd expect everyone to have finished. All the palace stewards and secretaries and the Duchess's lady's maids were there as usual, dressed in their neat, simple jewel-coloured suits and gowns – but Marco and the other entertainers from Master Xavier's troupe were nowhere to be seen.

Bianca went to the end of the table where platters of sliced breads, fruits, bowls of scrambled eggs and smoked meats were laid out, next to a huge steaming pot full of dark bitter coffee that was drunk from tiny black porcelain mugs.

Lady Amanita, the Duchess's private hairdresser, was just pouring herself a cup. She gave Bianca a friendly smile. Bianca liked Amanita – after all, they were both in the business of trying to get Duchess Catriona to sit still.

'Morning, Amanita,' Bianca said, picking up a plate and a crusty bread roll. 'Have you seen Marco?'

The smile faded from Amanita's lips. 'Oh my dear, didn't anyone tell you? The troupe is leaving.'

Bianca dropped her plate. It rattled on the table, and the bread roll fell off and bounced across the floor. 'Where are they?'

'The courtyard,' she said.' You'd better run if you want to catch them.'

Bianca turned and bolted out of the door.

She heard the commotion before she actually reached the courtyard – rattling boxes, creaking carts, stamping horses' hooves, the muttering of a crowd – and the Duchess Catriona's raised voice.

'No. I forbid it!'

Bianca stumbled out through an arch into the blazing sunshine and blinked, trying to get her head around the scene in front of her. It was true. Crates and trunks and boxes spilling over with costumes and props were being loaded onto seven carts emblazoned with *Master Xavier's Harlequin Troupe* in curly golden lettering. Master Xavier himself stood by the largest and grandest of them, politely defying the Duchess.

'My most heartfelt apologies, Your Highness,' he said, one hand clutched over his heart. 'But you have to understand – I run a travelling troupe, we must travel!'

Marco was sitting on the edge of the cart behind him, his shoulders hunched. He looked up and saw Bianca, sprang off the cart and ran across the square towards her.

'Is it true? Are you really leaving?' Bianca asked, dismay ringing in her voice.

Marco shrugged miserably. 'Father says this has been coming a long time. He set up the troupe to see the world, and that's what he plans to do – or at least some of the country outside La Luminosa. He doesn't want us to lose our edge and turn into lapdogs. Or something.'

'I . . . I don't want you to go.' The words seemed to tumble over each other all at once. 'You can't just go . . . you'll come back, right?'

'I hope so,' said Marco.

'I will never invite you to the palace again!' yelled the Duchess, stamping her foot.

'I hope that isn't true, Your Highness,' said Master Xavier, calmly. 'Marco,' he called. 'Come along, it's time.'

Bianca walked with Marco over to the cart. Master Xavier smiled at her.

'We'll be performing around the city for at least a few days,' he said kindly. 'And after that we'll take our act out to the vine country. Perhaps you could come and see us there.'

Bianca nodded, pressing her lips together, not quite trusting herself to speak.

Marco had helped her solve the mystery of di Lombardi's

death. He'd been the one person she could tell all her secrets, when she couldn't even trust Rosa or the other apprentices who she'd lived with for years. Plus, he'd even forgiven her for accusing him of being an assassin.

What's more, he was . . . like her. He was *normal*. It was oddly flattering to think that when he left, her best friend in the palace would be the Duchess, ruler of La Luminosa . . . but it was daunting, too. Bianca would never be Catriona's equal.

Bianca grabbed Marco and pulled him into a tight, brief hug and then pushed him away towards the steps of the cart. Marco climbed up with a grin. 'See you soon,' he said.

Bianca nodded.

Master Xavier climbed up too and swept a low, theatrical bow to Duchess Catriona. 'Goodbye, my Duchess.'

Duchess Catriona's face was pink with anger and she set her jaw, sullenly silent. Then one of the troupe struck up a cheerful march on a trumpet. The driver urged their horse forward, and the cart began to move off. The Duchess seemed torn for a second, her frown softening. Then she picked up her skirts and ran forward, calling after the cart. 'Come back soon, Master Xavier. You'll always be welcome here!'

Marco's father bowed again, and one by one the tumblers' carts rattled across the courtyard and out of the gate. Bianca ran to the edge of the bridge and watched as Marco's cart crossed the Grand Canal and vanished into the sparkling city.

The Duchess was calling to Bianca from behind her, but the sound seemed lost in the din of the morning markets and the glare of the bright bustling canals. It felt wrong that this should be just a normal day for all these people, going about their everyday business while Bianca's world had been pulled from under her. For a second, all she was aware of was the dull thumping of her heart. But then the full, catastrophic realisation hit her. Marco was gone.

Her best friend had left her.

Chapter Four

Bianca walked slowly across the courtyard, feeling as if her shoes were weighted with lead.

The Duchess stepped forward and took Bianca's hands in hers, squeezing them tight. 'I'm so sorry. I tried to forbid them to leave,' she said.

'I know.' Bianca nodded. She met the Duchess's eyes and gave the best smile she could muster. 'I just wish . . . I mean, first my master, and now . . .' She swallowed and shook her head. 'We'll see them again. They'll come back soon, won't they?'

Duchess Catriona nodded. 'I'll make sure they do. And you can go into the city to see them any time you like. In the meantime, you must see the other apprentices more often. You miss them, don't you?'

Bianca smiled, and this time she meant it. It was true – she hadn't had a chance to see Rosa, Cosimo, Domenico or Sebastiano since she moved to the palace.

'Your Highness,' said the thin, creaky voice of Secretary Franco. Duchess Catriona pulled a sour face as if she'd swallowed half a lemon and then turned to watch the

Secretary hurrying across the courtyard. 'Do you wish to change and prepare, before the reading of Master di Lombardi's will?'

'What are you trying to say?' asked Duchess Catriona, tossing her loose hair over her shoulder and smoothing down the ruffles in her skirt. 'I am perfectly prepared, thank you.'

'Then we should begin,' said Secretary Franco, and stood aside to let the Duchess lead the way inside. Bianca wanted to grab Catriona's hand and beg her to tell her all about the will reading afterwards, but she didn't want Franco to have any more reason to think of her as a disrespectful peasant. She stood back and looked down at the floor.

'Are you quite ready, Miss Bianca?' Secretary Franco croaked.

'Er . . . ready?' Bianca blinked at him.

'For the will reading. You should have received a summons as well.'

This came as a complete shock. Why would Bianca be asked to the will reading?

Duchess Catriona squeezed Bianca's arm. 'How wonderful! Master Annunzio has left you something!' she said. 'I wonder what it'll be?'

Bianca forced a smile, and let the Duchess lead her inside, but her heart thumped nervously in her chest. She knew that she wasn't Master di Lombardi's *least* favourite apprentice . . . she'd grown up in his house, abandoned on his doorstep. She didn't remember living anywhere else. And he'd always been very kind to her, in his gruff, grumpy way.

'I'm not sure,' Bianca said, lowering her voice. 'He only

gave me the paintbrush key because I happened to be there. I was just an apprentice!'

'And a cheeky one, too,' grinned Duchess Catriona as they ducked through the cool archway, flustered servants and courtiers stepping aside with bows and curtseys. 'He was always talking about some liberty you'd taken, how you wouldn't listen, how he didn't want you to grow up thinking natural talent would be enough . . .'

Bianca flushed. 'I disappointed him.'

'No . . . don't you see?' the Duchess went on, her voice softening. 'He was always talking about you.'

Bianca hadn't realised it was possible to blush deeper, but her cheeks were burning hot now. Perhaps di Lombardi *had* left her something. A few spare paints, perhaps? Not that she wanted anything. She had the secret passages and his own workshop, even if that was an accident – it was more than any apprentice could ask for.

But it would be nice to think he had spared a thought for her at some time.

The throne room doors swung open as if by magic when the Duchess approached – really Bianca knew that there were footmen standing on the other side, listening for her footsteps – and she swept in without breaking her stride. The small crowd inside broke off their conversations and knelt down, their hands over their hearts.

Bianca's spirits lifted as she saw that all of di Lombardi's other apprentices were there too. And so were Angela the kitchen maid, and Mistress Quinta, di Lombardi's cook and housekeeper. Bianca's blush faded and her grin grew wider as she realised that her master had included all his loyal servants in his will. She felt silly for thinking she was the only one. *Of course, the fate of the studio concerns all of us!*

Duchess Catriona swept up the steps to the golden throne in a rustle of silk while Bianca went to stand beside Cosimo, di Lombardi's head apprentice. There was a buzz of excited chatter as the apprentices greeted Bianca. Cosimo smiled and squeezed her hand, and Rosa pushed past him to gather Bianca into a hug.

'It's so good to see you,' Bianca whispered to them all. Sebastiano and Domenico grinned hugely over Rosa's shoulder.

The Duchess clapped her hands. Everyone fell silent and got to their feet.

'Master Cuocco,' said Duchess Catriona, settling on the throne. The Master Lawyer hurried to the foot of the steps and bowed, his thin white hair fluttering around his head like a halo. 'Let us begin,' she commanded.

Master Cuocco nodded, turned and accepted a scroll of paper from Secretary Franco – and then another, and another. He set them down on a table by his hand and coughed.

'On this day, the thirty-first of her eternal majesty's blessed reign, we the assembled gather at the Palace of La Luminosa, in the city of La Luminosa, to hear the final wishes of Master Annunzio di Lombardi. We gather in the sight of Her Eternal Majesty Duchess Catriona Sebastienne Cleolinda Vienna Regina da Luminosa . . .'

Bianca caught Duchess Catriona rolling her eyes and grinned. If this was the sort of thing where the Duchess was referred to by her full royal name, they were obviously going to be here for quite a while before anything really happened. She shuffled closer to the other apprentices and risked a wave over at Angela, who waved back.

'How's life at the palace?' Domenico whispered.

'Oh, it's . . . it's great,' Bianca said. 'It's kind of weird, though.'

'*Weird*?' Rosa gasped. 'Living in the palace, spending all your time with lords and ladies and walking arm in arm with the Duchess? I think you mean *fabulous*.'

Bianca smiled, but the wistful look in Rosa's eyes made her a little sad. Rosa would make a much better Royal-Artist-In-Residence than her. She wasn't, Bianca had to admit, a better artist – but she'd be better at enjoying the lavish lifestyle.

'I do have an amazing bedroom all to myself,' Bianca said. 'My bed is bigger than our whole room in Master di Lombardi's house!'

Rosa, Domenico and Sebastiano all groaned jealously.

'*Lucky*,' said Sebastiano. 'We're still in Filpepi's old house, sleeping in the dormitories with his apprentices.'

'It's better than before,' Rosa added hurriedly. 'They're all being much nicer. Poor things – to find out your master was a traitor! Such a shock. Still . . .' She leaned closer, with the intense gaze that Rosa always got when she had some really juicy gossip to pass on. 'They've been telling us terrible things about the way he ran his studio. No wonder they were all so on edge when we arrived.'

Bianca nodded, though she wasn't sure the other apprentices' behaviour could *all* be blamed on having a bad master.

Across the room Master Cuocco read out di Lombardi's gift to Mistress Quinta – a retirement fund that would keep her in comfort in her old age. The housekeeper fanned herself and turned away, trying to hide the tears that sprang into her eyes.

'And Cosimo and Lucia have even been working together!' Domenico went on.

'Well, it's our duty, as head apprentices,' said Cosimo sternly, though Bianca thought she caught the faintest hint of a blush. 'We have to keep everything working, until we know what's going to happen to our two studios.'

Rosa opened her mouth to speak, but then the words 'To my youngest apprentice, Bianca . . .' rang out across the throne room.

Bianca spun around to face Master Cuocco, who raised his eyebrow at her and then went back to reading.

'. . . I leave my favourite paintbrush.' Master Cuocco looked up at Bianca. 'I presume you know which one that is and can collect it for yourself?'

Bianca's stomach twisted and she nodded.

It's the one in my pocket.

But what did that mean? Did he always plan for her to find the secret passages? Why *her*?

'Good. *Ahem*. And I also leave her this letter and package.' Master Cuocco reached into a leather bag and pulled out an envelope and a small package, about the size of Bianca's fist, wrapped in thin black paper and tied with bright blue string. He held them out to her.

Bianca stepped forward and took them gingerly, almost

38

afraid that they would crumble or fly out of her hands. There, in Master di Lombardi's handwriting, was her name. She blinked back tears – inside this envelope there was a letter from Annunzio di Lombardi directly to her. She met the other apprentices' curious gazes and shrugged. She had no idea what he could want to say.

'Finally, and most importantly, my house and its contents, including my studio, unfinished works, the care and responsibility for all my current apprentices and servants, and the office of running my studio to the financial and creative benefit of the owner and the crown, are all left to . . .' Master Cuocco hesitated, and his eyes flickered to Duchess Catriona. 'Umm . . . my former apprentice . . . Master Piero Filpepi.'

A tense drawing in of breath echoed around the throne room, more like a hiss of collective pain than a gasp of shock.

Duchess Catriona got to her feet. 'Piero Filepi is a traitor to the crown,' she said in a low, slow growl, 'and as such, he cannot ever own any property in the city of La Luminosa.' She took a theatrical look out over the crowd. 'I declare that Master di Lombardi's studio and apprentices and . . . all of that stuff Master Cuocco listed . . . are now property of the crown. As Duchess, I will decide who will run them.'

There was a sigh as the assembled people let go of the breath they'd all been holding. Bianca grinned at the other apprentices. Thank goodness – now the Duchess could pick someone who could actually run the studio and get things back to normal.

'And I have made my decision,' said Duchess Catriona,

with a broad smile. Bianca looked up. Already? But who would it be? Most of the other artists in the city didn't have experience running a studio . . . they needed someone who already knew how it all worked, who'd been in charge of apprentices before.

'There is someone here who, while young, has certainly proved themselves.'

Bianca looked up at Cosimo. Cosimo had held them all together when their master had died. He'd kept the studio going when first di Lombardi and then Filpepi had gone.

'The studios will be run by someone who has worked hard to be worthy of inheriting Master di Lombardi's position.'

Cosimo's chest started to swell as he took a long breath. He deserved this.

'I refer, of course, to my court Artist-In-Residence. Bianca.'

Bianca was speechless. She gaped at the Duchess, who winked. Bianca could only blink dumbly back.

Master of the studio? Me? Bianca cast a look at the other apprentices and swallowed. They were all staring at her as if she'd turned into a frog in the middle of the throne room.

Cosimo looked like he'd been cast in stone. He spoke through gritted teeth, forcing a smile. 'Congratulations, Bianca. You're the Duchess's favourite.'

Bianca spun to face the Duchess. 'Your Highness,' she stammered, 'I can't . . . it's an honour that I don't . . .'

'It is my desire,' said Duchess Catriona, narrowing her eyes at the courtiers, who were looking just as shocked as the apprentices. 'And in case you've forgotten, my desire is your command. Now . . . please join me in congratulating Bianca.'

The Duchess nodded solemnly in Bianca's direction. Master Cuocco bowed, and the bobbing motion swept through the rest of the crowd as one by one everyone bowed or curtseyed to Bianca.

A huge pang of guilt lay heavy in her stomach. She tried to catch Cosimo's eye and shake her head, to tell him *I didn't ask for this, I don't want you all to bow to me!* But he averted his eyes as he and the other apprentices all bent their knees to her.

When they straightened up, he turned to Rosa and spoke in a low voice. 'We should return to the studio. We need to make sure everything's ready for our new master.'

The word *master* stung Bianca as much as if he'd called her a cheat and a thief outright.

The apprentices turned and filed slowly out of the room. Only Sebastiano briefly glanced back at Bianca, his eyes full of confusion and doubt, before Domenico nudged him and he turned away again.

Bianca started after them, but the Duchess's voice called her back. 'Mistress Bianca, wait a moment!'

Bianca flinched and then sighed. She couldn't ignore the Duchess. She turned and gave Catriona a weak smile.

'Well?' the Duchess asked, spreading her arms.

Bianca took a deep breath. Could she turn down the job? Maybe ask her to choose Cosimo instead? But how could she put it without angering the Duchess?

'Aren't you going to open it?' Duchess Catriona sat down on the throne and leaned forward eagerly. 'Come up here so I can see!'

Bianca looked down at her hands, still holding the envelope and the package wrapped in black paper. She'd almost forgotten them. It was hard to be quite as excited about her gifts from Master di Lombardi, now that she knew she was supposed to take his place. But she walked up the steps to the throne and sat on the floor at Duchess Catriona's feet to open them.

The bright blue string was silky under her fingers, and when she'd untied the parcel the black paper peeled away almost as soon as she breathed on it. Inside, something glinted.

Bianca gasped as she pulled out a gleaming medallion. It was an octagonal piece of obsidian set into an engraved silver circle, just the right size to fit into the palm of Bianca's hand. Bianca ran her finger around the eight sides of the obsidian and was fascinated at the way the light glinted purple and green in the depths of the dark stone.

'How beautiful,' the Duchess said softly.

Bianca threaded the bright blue silk string through the hole in the setting of the medallion and tied it around her neck.

'And the letter?' the Duchess asked, leaning forward, nosily.

Bianca opened the envelope and unfolded the sheet of yellowing paper. Her breath caught at the sight of Master di Lombardi's distinctive handwriting. But a moment later she exhaled a disappointed 'Oh'.

The letter was unreadable. Apart from the first words, the writing was just vague lines and squiggles, blurred together as if the letter had been left out in the rain. She read the four words that she could make sense of over and over, tears pricking at the corner of her eyes.

To my dear Bianca,

And then . . . nothing but a blur.

'Oh what a pity!' Duchess Catriona sat back. 'I'll have words with Master Cuocco about this. He should have checked.'

'No, it's . . . it's all right. I'm sure it's not his fault.' Bianca shook her head and held on tight to the medallion around her neck.

But it wasn't all right at all.

I'll never know what his final words to me would have been.

Chapter Five

The black panelled door is just ahead of me. Its bright blue edging seems to glow under the soft light from the torches that line the secret passages. I reach out and open the door, gazing out of the painted mural into the dark city.

When I've climbed through I pause in the small courtyard on the other side to turn and look up at the mural. It's a woman in grey, looking out of a window at a bright, stylised sun that doesn't cast any light. Its paint is slightly cracking, as if it was painted decades ago.

The courtyard seems neglected. An earth bed along one side is full of spiny, weedy-looking plants, and several of the cobblestones are cracked.

Pulling my shawl around myself against the cool night air, I walk out onto the road.

Despite the dark, starless sky, the streets are full of people. It feels like the middle of the day. The crowds criss-cross through the dim pools of light cast by candles in the windows and the crackling thunder-lamps on the ends of their tall poles, walking as easily as people in La Luminosa walk in the bright sunshine. They can obviously see as clearly in the dark as I can.

As I'm trying to decide which way to go, a flash of colour catches my eye, another one of the strange bright spots against the dark stone and the dark cloth of the people's clothes. This time it's a lady with a little black dog on the end of a bright rose-pink leather lead. Its hair is so long it drags along the ground. Its owner urges it on without giving me a second glance.

I decide to follow them, the pink lead flashing in and out of my sight as the dog weaves across the pavement in front of the lady's dark skirts. I keep a respectful distance. I wonder where they're going.

The dog lady leads me around a corner, the buildings draw back and I find myself at the edge of a large open square, a lot like the Piazza del Fiero. Black and white cobblestones are laid out in a pattern of swirling lines and circles. They flow from the centre of the square, where a tall statue of a man stands surrounded by a bed of beautiful flowers that appear to be glowing from within.

I cross the square and gaze at the flowers. They look like bright white tulips, shaped like little lanterns on the ends of long black stems. They really are glowing! They seem familiar. I'm sure I'm supposed to know their name . . . but I can't quite put my finger on it.

Then I glance up at the statue and laugh out loud.

'Master!'

The man on the tall plinth is unmistakably Annunzio di Lombardi. Except instead of being old and stooped, he's middle-aged, tall and strong-looking. The statue is made of black stone, apart from a bright gold circlet on his head.

I walk around the plinth until I find some writing, engraved and embossed with the same gold that gleams on di Lombardi's head.

> *Annunzio di Lombardi*
> *From the people of Oscurita*
> *He will never be forgotten*

'Oscurita . . .' I smile, enjoying the feel of the name on my lips.

I turn away from the statue and set off down another street, following a man with bright yellow stars embroidered on his tunic. We cross a bridge over the dark canal and I stop for a few minutes to watch the reflections of the hundreds of candles in the windows of the buildings glittering in the water. I nod to a pair of guards dressed in glinting silver armour engraved with swirling patterns like the trails of ink in water.

Walking alongside the canal, I find a little group of peddlers' stalls. They seem to sell anything and everything – silver jewellery, books, birds in cages and strange-looking food and drink.

I stop by a stall that sells fruit, though it's not like any fruit that grows in La Luminosa. One is the shape of a pear, but has the deep red colour of ripe strawberries, and when I reach out gingerly to touch the surface, it's fuzzy and soft like a peach. I pick it up and give it a very gentle squeeze. I bet it's juicy and delicious.

My mouth waters. But I haven't got any money, or any

way to barter for the beautiful fruit. I can't help myself as I bring the fruit to my mouth and take a bite. Sweet juice flows into my mouth – it tastes like pears, peaches and strawberries all mixed together. It's the most delicious thing I've ever eaten.

'Oi!'

I look up just in time to duck as the peddler leans over the stall and makes a grab for my shoulder.

'Little thief!' the peddler yells, shoving a customer aside, marching out from behind the cart.

I back away, my cheeks burning. 'I'm so sorry . . . I . . .' I toss the fruit back at the peddler, turn and launch into a run.

'Guards!' the peddler shouts. The crowd joins in the cry as I pound along the canalside. 'Guards, thief! Stop her!'

Glancing back, I catch a flash of glinting silver as the guards on the bridge begin to run after me; I put on a burst of speed. A pair of men in heavy clanking armour will never outrun me! The next bridge isn't guarded and I sprint up and over it, ducking into the first alley I see on the other side.

Eventually my breath starts to rasp painfully in my throat and I stagger to a stop. A stitch stabs into my side and I gasp and lean against a wall.

I look around, intrigued. This seems like a more expensive part of the city – it's a lot like the part of La Luminosa where Filpepi's studio was, with its big houses set back from the road. The closest one has a garden in front of it, just like Filpepi's, where trees bend their branches together to form an arch – though these trees aren't the flowering orange trees that grow in La Luminosa. They're thin, black-barked and without leaves, more like wrought-iron statues than real plants.

Angela once told me the best cure for a stitch was to keep walking, so I clamp my hand to my side and take a few steps down the road, hoping that by doubling back I will avoid the guards. I want to see the statue of di Lombardi again, and I wonder if I can find it – or if maybe the city will arrange itself for me so I stumble across it? I set off, guessing which way the square must be.

But as I round a corner, half-expecting to find myself on the edge of the square, or at least back in the maze of streets and canals near the abandoned courtyard, I look up and see something quite amazing.

On the other side of a wide, black canal looms a magnificent castle. A bridge leads to the main gate, and banners flutter from its towers, just like the Palace of La Luminosa. But instead of the logical, geometric towers and courtyards of the palace, this castle is as thin and dark as one of the black trees in the garden – it seems to meander upwards, little round towers springing off the central building at random. The lightning in the thunder-lamps here casts flickering blue and green shadows between the dark stones, and the roof glitters an oily blue-green-black colour. The banners carry an eight-pointed silver star on a background of deep purple.

I gape at the castle, stunned by the strange beauty of it. And there's something else . . . it seems so familiar. As if I've been here, or dreamed this before. I have to get inside! I can almost see the twisting corridors and spiral staircases, curved alcoves, carved black wood doors.

But before I can take a step towards the bridge over the canal, two heavy hands land on my shoulders. Twisting, I try to get away, but it's no good.

'Got you, you little thief!' The peddler from the fruit stall yanks me around to face him, grinning smugly. The two guards are behind him, their silver armour glinting and their faces stern.

'This is the girl?' one says, grabbing my arm so tightly that I wince, but I can't pull it away without twisting it right out of my shoulder.

'Yeah, that's the one!'

I flush with shame. I want to explain that I've never done anything like that before – I don't know why I did it now – but I get the feeling that trying to explain won't end well.

'Off to the dungeons with you,' says the other guard, and pushes me forward so I stumble over my own feet. But I don't feel cross, or even very scared, despite the ache in my arm and the wicked-looking obsidian blades on the end of the guards' spears. Oddly, I just feel pleased – after all, I wanted to see the inside of the castle, and now I'm going to!

I put up no resistance as the guards drag me over the bridge, across the main courtyard and through a small, dark archway into a dim passage that seems to curve down in a long, smooth spiral.

The passage suddenly opens up on one side and I can see into a large courtyard. A flash of deep blue catches my eye as we pass, and I gasp.

The Baron da Russo. He's standing there, wearing his black cloak with the blue trim showing as it folds over his shoulder.

He doesn't see me – he's bowing low to a lady in a purple dress embroidered with twisting veins of black and silver.

The guards steer me on. Wrenching myself out of the guards' grip, I spin to run back to the courtyard. The Baron is still there. This time I notice the woman's crown, a delicate silver tiara studded with tiny diamonds that glimmer like stars when she moves. And her face . . . there's something familiar about it. Her dark brown hair is smooth and glossy and caught up in an elaborate twist over one shoulder, but if it was loose and messy, and she was about twenty-five years younger . . .

I frown. The woman looks a lot like *me*.

I start to yell a warning, but the guard clamps his hand over my mouth and drags me away. I flail my arms, trying to grab on to a plinth in a stone alcove to stop the guards from dragging me along the passage, but my fingers curl around something that comes away in my hand. The guards hold me tight between them and shove me forward, but now I let them. I'm looking down at the thing I've picked up. It's a bracelet, with engraved flowers twining around the surface and a clasp – but it's tiny, as if it was made for a baby. As I look at it, my hand tingles, and then the tingling gets worse and worse – terrible pins and needles sending shooting twinges up my arm . . .

And then Bianca woke up.

The piercing light of sunrise was falling on her face and the sky outside the window was awash with pink and gold.

Bianca wriggled and turned over. Her right hand was still

tingling and she flexed her fingers underneath her pillow. She sighed, and it turned into a yawn. She must have been asleep for hours, but she was exhausted, as if she had really been running around a city all night. If only the Baron hadn't appeared again, it would have been a good adventure.

She felt so at home there – *Oscurita*, she remembered with a smile. It was a good name. It felt as if she'd known it all her life.

There was still an odd, cold feeling in the fingers of her right hand. She must've numbed it during the night by lying on it for too long. She sat up and brought it out from under the pillow.

Something glinted, tucked between her fingers. She froze, her heart suddenly hammering. Slowly, she raised the little silver bracelet so it caught the pink dawn rays. It was the child's bracelet, the one she'd seen in the dark city . . . in Oscurita. It'd left an imprint of twining flowers across the inside of her fingers where she'd been clutching it.

'It wasn't a dream,' Bianca whispered, turning the bracelet round and round in her fingers. She could only have been sleepwalking – but then how did she get back here? Excitement fluttered in her stomach. What if it was some kind of . . . magic? Did this mean there was a real lady with a face like Bianca's? Did it mean the Baron da Russo was with her, weaving her into his web of lies and treachery? Terror shot through her.

I have to get back. I have to warn her!

But how do you get back to a place that's only half real?

The sun rose and glowed more fiercely in the sky as Bianca painted furiously, dipping her brush again and again into her palette of black, grey and blue paint. First she sketched out the lines of an Oscurita building, with a doorway and a thunder-lamp crackling in a window. Then she laid down blocks of colour, patterns of light and shade – mostly shade. The maid knocked and walked in, intending to get Bianca's clothes ready for the day, but Bianca waved her away. She was adding some of the details now, the lights and the blue shadows. She uncorked a tiny vial of *lux aurumque*, the glowing golden oil that added the final, magic ingredient to any paint, and quickly mixed up an *ether*. As the paint turned transparent in the copper bowl, Bianca smiled to herself, amazed at how quickly she'd mastered some of di Lombardi's magical paints.

The great bell of the palace chapel led a chorus of church bells from all over the city just as Bianca finished painting the *ether* onto the handle. She felt it swell and turn solid under her brush. It was ten o'clock: she'd missed breakfast, and she really ought to be getting over to Filpepi's studio, to start her first day as Mistress Bianca.

She held up the magical paintbrush and whispered, 'Hidden rooms, secret passages, second city.' The paintbrush unfolded its secret key and she slipped it into the painted lock. 'Come on, come on. Take me back to Oscurita,' she whispered.

The door opened, but it wasn't the dark city on the other side. Sighing, she pushed the door wide. She'd created another entrance into the secret passages. A few days ago she would have been cartwheeling with joy – but now, all she really felt was foolish.

I was stupid to think it would be that easy. Bianca closed the painted door, lifted the canvas from the easel and then threw a dustsheet over it.

She shook herself. She had things to do today – behave like a master artist. She hadn't asked for this duty, but the Duchess herself had given it to her. She couldn't just abandon it for a world she'd only seen in her dreams. She tugged the strings of her bodice tight and knotted them behind her back. It was her first day as the head of both of the greatest studios in La Luminosa, and she was already late.

Chapter Six

The other apprentices were there when she walked in, chatting and preparing their paints and canvases. Bianca plastered a friendly smile on her face.

'Hi everyone,' she said.

Cosimo and Lucia exchanged a look and then they both stood and bowed to her.

Bianca looked around at the other apprentices, searching for support . . . and found none. She didn't blame Cosimo or Lucia if they hated her – both of them were head apprentices, either could have taken over the studios and done a much better job of it than she could. But the rest of di Lombardi's apprentices wouldn't even look at her, and Filpepi's were staring at her with undisguised anger.

'What can we do for you, Mistress?' Lucia said. Her voice was smooth but there were daggers in it.

'Do you think she knows what time it is?' whispered a girl's voice. Bianca's gaze fell on Gabriella, who'd folded her arms and turned away to whisper to Francesca. Bianca's heart sank even more. Gabriella had never liked her – she'd never liked any of di Lombardi's apprentices. The idea that

Bianca, the youngest, was in charge must be killing her.

'I'm sorry about –' Bianca began, but Lucia interrupted, turning on Gabriella.

'Gabriella, silence!' she snapped.

Bianca clenched her fists in the ends of her sleeves. 'Lucia, it's all ri—'

Lucia marched over to Gabriella and knocked down her folded arms. 'Mistress Bianca is our master now. She can come and go as she pleases, and you have no right to scold her for it!' Her tone was vicious.

Bianca flushed, stung by the spite in Lucia's voice. But she gave them the friendliest grin she could. 'Listen, I'm sorry about this, and I'm sorry for being late,' she said, spreading her hands. 'But all I'm going to do is manage things, not interfere with your work or anything – I trust you to do the work just like you always did. Nothing's really going to change. You don't have to act like I'm Master di Lombardi!'

'Of course not, Mistress,' said Lucia, with a smile that was all teeth and no warmth.

'Yes, it's *so kind* of you to say you trust us,' muttered Gennaro.

'I didn't mean . . .' Bianca began, but then she stopped herself. Fine. Maybe they wouldn't listen to anything she said. Well, then, she'd just have to show them she meant it.

'Do you all have work to do?' she asked. 'Does anyone need anything from me?'

Cosimo and Lucia exchanged another look – this time accompanied by matching sly smiles. They both turned and picked up huge, teetering stacks of paper from the workbenches behind them.

'These are all Master di Lombardi's papers about the studio,' said Cosimo, shoving them into Bianca's arms.

'And these are Filpepi's,' said Lucia, plonking hers down on top. Bianca staggered under the weight and pressed her chin on top of the stack to stop them sliding off onto the floor. She gave Cosimo a pleading look, but he returned it with a blank stare.

Lucia rolled her eyes. '*Not* that I have *years* of experience in basically *running* this studio while our master was busy plotting with the Baron da Russo, or anything,' she said. 'But I think the master is supposed to know everything that's being worked on and make sure it's all on time and up to scratch.'

'Right. Thanks,' Bianca said, though she didn't feel particularly thankful. She staggered over to the nearest workbench and put down the huge piles of paper.

'I think the master of the studio should use the master's office,' said Lucia.

Bianca thought about that dim room, with all Filpepi's things still crowded around the desk, and shuddered. She didn't want to vanish upstairs and sit there all by herself. If she did that she'd never have the chance to talk to the other apprentices and prove to them that she wasn't trying to take di Lombardi's place.

Well, she thought, *she did say I was in charge.*

'Actually, I think I'll work in here,' she said brightly. 'I'll pull a table into a corner so I'm not in anyone's way.'

Lucia's eyes glinted unpleasantly and her nostrils flared,

but she swept Bianca another low bow. 'As you like, Mistress Bianca,' she muttered. As she straightened up, she turned to Cosimo and hissed 'I told you so!'

Cosimo glanced back at Bianca. She'd expected him to be angry – but he just looked sad, which was so much worse.

Bianca sat down on a stool and stared up at the pile of papers.

This is going to be a long, long day.

Bianca rubbed her eyes. Poring over the tiny, spidery handwriting on the studio documents had made them dry and sore – but at least now she had an idea where to start. She got up from her stool, stretched and headed over to the easel where Rosa was working.

'Rosa, it says here you're working on the commission for the Cathedral.'

'Yes,' said Rosa. She stepped aside to let Bianca look at the painting. It was a huge landscape, as tall as a carthorse and nearly twice as long, showing a group of pilgrims making their way through a valley bathed in golden light. Bianca examined it.

'Great,' she said. 'This is really good work. But, um . . . it's due to be delivered tomorrow. Do you . . . do you think it'll be finished in time to dry overnight?'

'I don't know,' said Rosa flatly.

'Oh – OK,' Bianca said. Everyone was looking at her now, like they were expecting her to say something. *I hate this*, she thought. *I can't tell Rosa what to do. She's like my big sister!*

Well, you have to.

'I think, I mean, would you mind moving on to the magical paints now?'

'I'd love to,' said Rosa, 'but I can't.'

'Why?'

'We haven't got any,' Francesca blurted out. 'We used all the ones that'd been mixed and we don't know how to make more.' Gabriella and Ezio glared at her as if she'd spoiled the punchline of a joke. Bianca felt her blood warming her cheeks, but she forced herself to smile.

'Oh no! I'm sorry, I didn't realise.' She took a deep breath, but couldn't help adding, 'If you need something you should tell me.'

'We wouldn't dream of telling the master how to do her job,' said Lucia.

'Anyway, it's not like we can make more ourselves!' Domenico said.

'Master di Lombardi never taught anyone but you,' agreed Sebastiano, in a quiet voice.

Bianca felt sick. All those times di Lombardi had pulled her away to give her extra lessons and show her how to make the magic oils do what she wanted, she'd felt so pleased with herself. So *special*. She'd had no idea it could put her in a position like this. She looked up at Cosimo, desperate to tell him she was sorry, that she didn't *force* their master to teach her. He turned away, painting the eyelashes onto a portrait with deliberate care and a stony face.

'I . . . I thought he must have at least left instructions,' Bianca said. 'In case . . .'

The blank looks on Rosa and Domenico's faces told her she was wrong.

'But Lucia, didn't Filpepi ever –'

Lucia gave Bianca a look of disdain that could've stopped a bolting horse. 'Filpepi? Share his secrets? Filpepi the traitor?'

'Well, I'll have to teach you,' Bianca said. She was gratified to see that Gabriella looked surprised. *You really thought I'd rather the techniques were lost?* 'But there's no time now. Get on with what you're doing and I'll make up new batches of everything we need. Lucia, where did Filpepi do his mixing?'

'The supplies and the equipment are both in that room there,' said Lucia, pointing to a closed door, and smiling slyly. 'But it's locked, and we've lost the key.'

Lost the key, or hidden it?

Bianca turned slowly to look at all the apprentices, her fists clenching.

Do none of you care at all? she wanted to scream. *Do you all hate me so much that you'd rather destroy Master di Lombardi's legacy than see me in charge?*

She tried to count to ten while taking a deep breath, and made it as far as six before she scooped up a marble sculpture of a man about the length of her arm and carried it over to the door. Hefting it so his outstretched hands were pointing down, she slammed them into the wood around the lock again and again until the door splintered and creaked open.

She set the marble man down carefully on the floor and turned to the others, who were standing frozen, with their mouths open. 'I'll be inside if anyone needs me.' She walked inside and slammed the door behind her.

* * *

Bianca half-expected the apprentices to have vanished when she came out of the room again a couple of hours later, heaving a basket full of sloshing paint pots. But they were all still there, working on their paintings.

'Here we go,' she said, emptying the basket onto the workbench, pot by pot. 'I've made two *ethers*, and here's a *glimmer*, a *shimmer,* a *glitter* – no, sorry, that's the *luce stellare*, *that* one's the *glitter*, don't get them confused – and there's a *saltatio,* a *respirare*, and an *animare*. Rosa, can you –'

The lunch bell in the kitchen jangled, cutting Bianca off. She sighed as the apprentices filed out, without waiting to be dismissed – all except Rosa, who was staring sadly at the faint glow of the *animare* as it swished around inside the pot like a living creature.

'I'd better stay and make a start on the pilgrims,' she muttered. 'It's going to be late if we don't keep working.'

Bianca smiled and shook her head. 'No, it's all right, I'll stay and start it myself. I'll get some lunch when you come back.'

Rosa grinned at Bianca, and then her cheeks flushed slightly. 'Sorry we've all been . . . you know. It's childish. I'm sure we'll get over it.'

Bianca grinned back, feeling like a ten-tonne marble statue had been lifted off her shoulders. 'Thanks, Rosa.'

Rosa squeezed Bianca's shoulder and hurried off after the others. Bianca hopped up onto the stool in front of the easel, and felt even more of the tension melt away. She hadn't even taken out her brush yet, but just sitting in front of a painting getting ready to start work felt like a huge relief. She wasn't desperately trying to please the Duchess – or find a way back to the dark city – she was just doing what she loved.

She studied the figures of the pilgrims. They were really good – a fine lady in green on a white horse rode with a fat white-robed priest by her side. Even though the figures were small, Bianca could tell they were deep in conversation just from the subtle lines of their faces. Behind them a pair of ponies carried bulging saddlebags, and then a young man in a blue uniform rode with a young woman in practical brown leather.

Rosa definitely had an eye for painting people. Now Bianca just needed to add a little magic.

She traced the lines of movement with her dry paintbrush for a few minutes, not adding paint but visualising the ways the people might move. Then she carefully unscrewed the top from the pot of *animare* and dipped her paintbrush in. The paint swirled and moved on the hairs of the brush, as if it couldn't wait to get onto the painting. Bianca chewed her lip as she worked – this was fine detail, and undoing it would be a real pain. She started small: a swoosh along the jaw of the lady to make her head tilt back and forward, a few swipes along the horses' legs in a careful rhythm made them move up and down as if they were trotting along the road.

The pilgrims slowly but surely came to life as Bianca painted. A smile came and went on the priest's chubby face; the soldier at the back nodded to his companion; the saddlebags on the ponies swayed back and forth. After a while, Bianca's stomach grumbled and she sat back to take it all in. It wasn't the elaborate lifelike movement her master would have been able to add, but it was pretty good for an hour's work!

Bianca was so pleased that she even smiled at Lucia as she passed her in the corridor on the way to the kitchen. Lucia smiled back, which gave Bianca a stab of worry deep in her stomach . . . but she was starving, and whatever Lucia was planning for her next, it could wait until after she'd eaten.

'What's for lunch, Angela?' Bianca greeted the kitchen girl with a broad smile.

Angela returned her a look of surprise. 'Well, it *was* omelettes with sweet pepper and spiced sausage . . .'

Bianca's mouth watered, but her face fell. 'Was?'

'Lucia said you weren't coming,' Angela said in a small voice. 'I'm so sorry – it must've been a mix-up. We've just given the leftovers to the cat! I would make you another, only we're out of eggs . . .'

'No, no, it's fine,' Bianca sighed, looking down at the scruffy white and ginger cat as it wolfed down the last of the bright red and yellow omelette. 'I'd better get back to work.'

Here we go again . . .

Bianca hurried back down the corridor, her feet slapping hard on the black-and-white tiled floor, a ball of apprehension starting to grow in her gut. Just how many times was Lucia going to do something like this before she got used to the idea of Bianca being in charge?

Bianca made herself slow down and walk casually into

the studio, determined not to give them the satisfaction of seeing her run. At first, she breathed a sigh of relief to see that the apprentices were all in their places and nothing was actually on fire – then she looked at the Cathedral painting and felt sick. Something – someone – had brushed against the magical paint before it was dry, and now the pilgrims were swaying back and forth lifelessly like marionettes dangling from their strings on the front of a puppeteer's stall.

Unenchanting the painting would take hours of meticulous work – more than twice the time that adding the magic had taken.

'Oh, *come on*!' she wailed. 'Who did this? There's no way we can deliver this on time now! I want to know who it was.' Bianca looked at Francesca. *Come on, I trust you – mostly – just tell me the truth . . .*

But Francesca just stared at the floor.

'Well, fine, but I want this cleared up as soon as possible. Sebastiano, come and help Rosa; you can work on stripping the *animare* together, and then –'

'Rosa can manage,' said Cosimo. 'Sebastiano, the background for the Count d'Oro's portrait still needs finishing, you stay where you are.'

'But – but this needs to be done quickly!' Bianca said. 'I really think he should help Rosa.'

'Cosimo's right,' Lucia put in.

Bianca clenched her fists. It wouldn't help at all to yell *And who asked you?!* at the top of her lungs . . .

Sebastiano looked from Bianca to Cosimo to Lucia, cringing like a mouse cornered by a pack of feral cats, and followed Cosimo's instruction. He turned back to the Count's portrait.

Bianca's shoulders slumped. *I give up*, she thought. *Maybe they'll come round, maybe they won't – but I won't stay here and fight them all day!* 'I'm going to work in Filpepi's study,' she muttered, and walked out of the studio. When she reached the dim upstairs room, she carefully arranged the papers on Filpepi's desk so that it looked like she was working on the commission schedule. Then she pulled out the paintbrush key and approached the painting of the ancient ruined chapel that hung on the wall beside the desk. She felt a stab of loss, remembering when she and Marco climbed through it, discovering the fake Duchess's wedding dress enchanted out of its painting. Fighting back her emotions, Bianca took a deep, steadying breath. She clambered through the stone door in the painting and closed it behind her without looking back.

Chapter Seven

Bianca wandered aimlessly through the passages for a little while, peering through the painted windows in some of the doors, trying to puzzle out where their paintings were in the real city. The anger and humiliation she felt at the hands of Gabriella and Lucia was still fresh, and she needed a distraction. She saw the bright glistening waters of the canal through one painting, and the inside of a cosy sitting room through the next. Down another turning there was a church mural, and then one she thought she'd helped paint years ago, in the San Giulietta orphanage.

How did Master di Lombardi ever navigate all these doors? I ought to try to make a map. But she couldn't muster much enthusiasm for the idea right now. It just didn't feel the same exploring the passages on her own. She stopped to examine di Lombardi's strange symbols on the outside of the paintings and suddenly missed Marco so intensely she could almost feel it burning in the back of her throat. She pictured him running between the painted doors taking note of the strange characters – he'd been determined to decode them.

He'd never treat her the way her so-called friends in the studio had . . .

What's more, I can't tell Duchess Catriona about any of it – not if I don't want her throwing a fit and threatening to sack them.

Bianca recognised a religious painting of men kneeling in worship, and to one side was a barred wooden door. Realisation struck her: she had been through it before. On the other side was the Church of Santa Cecilia. She recalled Marco helping her stumble through with di Lombardi after the fire in his studio. Bianca couldn't help opening the door an inch, spotting stained glass windows which cast coloured light onto an altar. The church was miles from the palace, but could be reached in minutes through the passageways.

She closed the door of the painting and ducked back into the passage, her jaw set in resolve. An idea that had been niggling at the back of her mind seemed suddenly to spring into focus. If these paintings led anywhere in the city, maybe she could find Marco!

She began to search the paintings methodically, peering through every door that had a window or that she dared open just a crack. She knew she might not find Master Xavier's troupe – even though Master di Lombardi's enchanted paintings were all over the city and she was sure there were some in the estates outside the city walls, it wasn't very likely they'd actually be standing in front of one. But she kept looking, pleased with the distraction. It was still thrilling to realise that she was travelling all over La Luminosa while only moving a few feet at a time.

Then, suddenly, just as Bianca was closing a door that'd opened into an opulent empty bedroom, something caught her eye. She hesitated, and then opened the door a little way again. She was sure she'd seen the name Xavier somewhere in this room! She looked around at the sapphire-coloured quilted blanket on the bed, the thick white sheepskins on the wooden floor, the polished silver mirror on the dressing table . . .

There! Propped up against one of the drawers, Bianca could see a printed poster emblazoned with the words:

MASTER XAVIER'S MARVELLOUS
HARLEQUIN TROUPE
GASP! AT THE FEATS OF TUMBLING
ACROBATICS!
HEAR! THE GREAT STORIES OF THE AGE!
SEE! THE HARLEQUIN TRIUMPH AGAINST
THE WICKED DUKE!
SHOWS TWICE DAILY: PIAZZA DA FERRANTI

'*Yes!*' Bianca said, jumping on the spot.

'Who's there?' A lady's voice rang out from the other side of the bedroom door. Bianca leapt back, pulling the painted door shut with a soft *thud* just as she heard the bedroom door creak open. She listened for a while: the voice said 'Hello? Zola, is that you?' and she heard feet crossing the room to the window and back, then the sound of the door shutting again.

Phew! Bianca grinned. That was a close call – but now she

knew exactly where Marco and his troupe would be. Her heart felt ten times lighter as she hurried along the passages. She soon found herself looking out through the mural on the outside wall of the Horse and Apples, a restaurant on one corner of the Piazza del Ferranti. Thin beams of light poured into the dim secret passages through the cracks in the old barn door and as Bianca looked through she could see the swishing tails of the horses in the painting.

Her eyes adjusted to the brightness and she saw that it was safe to slip out – there was a big crowd assembled in the Piazza, but they were all facing away from the Horse and Apples, towards the makeshift stage that'd been put up outside the master blacksmith's workshop. Bianca smiled as she saw familiar figures in sea-creature and mermaid costumes dancing and tumbling. She swiftly unlocked the door, crossed the few feet of magical straw-covered space and hopped out onto the warm stones of the Piazza.

Bianca hurried around the edge of the crowd, looking for the backstage area, as the audience gasped and applauded each time one of the performers sprang onto another's shoulders or turned a somersault in the air. Bianca paused, her heart in her mouth, as the harlequin in his black and red diamond costume started to climb a tall pole on one side of the stage. She looked up and her stomach twisted – a tightrope wire was strung high above the stage, between the pole and the roof of the neighbouring smithy.

'Ladies, gentlemen, knights and squires,' the harlequin called out, balancing with one foot on the top of the pole. 'Throw us a penny and we'll walk this wire!'

The mermaids sitting at the front of the stage unfurled a long strip of glistening green and blue silk, and a steady rain of pennies started to shower into it, making it ripple like the surface of the sea.

The harlequin started his slow-quick-slow walk, back and forth against the high wire, wobbling far more than looked safe but somehow never falling. Bianca stopped to watch for a second, until she dragged her gaze away. The show was wonderful, but it wasn't why she was here.

There was a curtain strung up over the master blacksmith's shop door with a sign pinned to it, painted in black on red cotton: BACKSTAGE, KEEP OUT. Bianca grinned and ducked through.

The whole smithy had apparently been taken over by the troupe – boxes and trunks overflowing with costumes and props vied for space with the dangling collections of iron tools, pokers, shovels, gleaming flint-sharp scissors and horseshoes. Another curtain had been strung up across the centre of the room to form a makeshift dressing room. Actors and tumblers were milling about, chatting, painting their faces or struggling in and out of costumes.

'Hey, no audience backstage! Oh, it's you,' said a voice, and Bianca turned and looked up into the smiling face of Master Xavier. 'Welcome, Mistress Bianca. Are you enjoying the show?'

Bianca grinned up at him, but before she could say it was wonderful, a voice rang out from behind the curtain:

'Bianca?' Marco stepped forward, beaming. His face was painted, half red and half black, with a diamond over each eye, and he was wearing a smaller version of the harlequin's costume. Bianca ran over and stopped just short of grabbing him into a hug.

'Can you talk?' she asked. 'Do you have to go on stage?'

Marco's face fell. 'Well, I . . . I'm not . . .'

'You've got a few minutes,' said Master Xavier. 'The doppelgänger doesn't enter until after the Fire Twins have finished their routine. I'll call you.'

'Right. Thanks.' But Marco didn't look at all relieved. Master Xavier gave Marco a stiff nod, then walked away to watch the stage through the curtain.

'What's wrong?' Bianca asked. Marco's expression only became more miserable.

'I'm just . . .' He cast an apprehensive glance over towards the stage and beckoned for her to come inside the makeshift dressing room. Bianca followed him through the curtain. The unlit furnace took up most of the space, but it'd been turned into a make-up table and held a large mirror, a scattered rainbow of greasepaint pots and piles of costume jewellery. Marco slumped against the furnace and folded his arms. 'I don't know if they're going to want me much longer.'

'What?' Bianca gasped. 'But your father . . .'

Marco lifted one hand to rub it across his cheek, but stopped himself before smearing his greasepaint. 'It's the high wire. I can't do it. Every time I try, I just get this . . .' He shrugged. 'Ech, it's stupid.'

'No, go on.' Bianca hopped up so she was sitting on the huge, cold iron anvil beside Marco.

Marco gave a deep sigh. 'Remember the fire?'

'Yeah,' Bianca said simply. She didn't think either of them would ever forget it: the fire that Filpepi had set to kill di Lombardi. The fire that had destroyed her home.

'I was up on that roof,' Marco blurted. 'There was all the fire and smoke below and I couldn't climb back up to the window and the roof – the roof was getting hotter and hotter . . .'

Bianca remembered. The copper-tiled roof had been like a burning island in a river of black smoke and flickering flame.

'So,' Marco said, with a miserable shrug. 'It's stupid. But every time I get up on the high wire, it's like I'm back there. I smell smoke and I can't see properly, and my feet start to feel like they're burning. I can't do it, I –'

'Marco!' Marco flinched as his father pushed through the curtain. 'It's your cue.' He glanced at Bianca and then laid a heavy hand on Marco's shoulder. 'You'll be fine when you get up there.'

Bianca wanted to think so too, but Marco had gone pale as a ghost. He looked more likely to throw up than anything else.

'I'll be here,' she said. She grabbed his hand and squeezed it hard for a second. 'I'll be in the crowd – you can look at me and that'll tell you that it's fine and we both got out of the fire. OK?'

Marco nodded, but didn't look any less frightened. He headed for the stage like a man being led to the gallows, and Bianca ran outside and pushed through the crowd in the baking sunshine of the Piazza right to the front of the stage.

Up on the high wire, the harlequin was applauding from

71

one side as the Lotti sisters twirled their flaming staves and bowed, then ran nimbly across the high wire, dropped the staves, flaming end first, into buckets of water on the stage and slid down the pole. The audience whooped and cheered.

The actor playing the Wicked Duke swept onstage in a dramatic rustle of black and blue. The audience booed and jeered, and the Duke threw back his cloak to reveal Marco, standing with his head and arms hanging limp. 'Now that stupid harlequin's tricks will end forever – I will replace him with my own harlequin, and then nobody will know I'm the one pulling the strings!' At a sweeping gesture from the Duke, Marco seemed to come alive. He bowed to the audience, who booed even more – but laughed, too – and, after a pause that only Bianca saw, started to climb up the pole.

With every step, Bianca's heart beat a little faster. Was it her imagination, or did his hand shake before he grabbed the next rung? She willed him forward, wringing her hands in front of her. The crowd applauded again as he reached the top of the pole, turned to bow . . . and wobbled. The crowd gasped. Bianca's hand flew to her mouth, and then she forced herself to lower it again and smile up at Marco. She had to show him she believed in him, even if he couldn't believe in himself.

Marco straightened up slowly. He seemed to be scanning the crowd – was he looking for Bianca? *I'm here!* she thought, turning her face up to the light, but she didn't dare distract him by waving or shouting. Marco's hands were shaking, but his legs seemed steady as he took one step forwards onto the high wire. It bent a little under his weight and he took another step, and then another. The Wicked Duke climbed swiftly up the pole after him. Marco raised his hand with a flourish. *He's going to do it!* Bianca grinned. *He's going to be –*

But then Marco's chest heaved and his knees gave way. Bianca gripped the front of the stage, ready to spring up and try to catch him, but Marco didn't fall – he just crouched on the wire, clinging on with his fingers and toes. A drop of sweat fell from his face and splashed on the stage in front of Bianca.

The harlequin raised his hands and turned to the crowd. 'Ha-ha! No silly puppet could walk the tightrope like I do! Get back to your master!' And with that, he hurried along the wire to Marco, bent down and lifted him to his feet. He thrust him back along the wire. Marco flailed, his arms windmilling at his sides, but the Wicked Duke caught him securely, shook his fist at the harlequin and then hooked Marco's belt onto the rope and lowered him down to the stage.

The audience roared with laughter and applauded as Marco's feet hit solid ground. Marco's face was white. He dipped his head in an attempt at a bow, and then turned and staggered offstage, pushing past Bianca and through the curtain. Bianca hurried after him.

Marco dived into the dressing area and Bianca followed, in time to see him kick the furnace hard. He yelped and hopped on one foot for a second, then sank down on the anvil.

'They knew I couldn't do it!' he said. 'They had a whole

bit worked out to rescue me!' He hung his head and let out a long growl of disappointment.

'I'm sure they –' Bianca began.

'No. I know what they're saying. A tumbler who's scared of heights is useless. Go on.' He gestured to the curtain. 'Look.'

Bianca didn't want to, but she couldn't help herself – she peeked through the curtain into the rest of the shop. Marco's father, Olivia and two more actors were standing in a little group, talking with their heads bowed together. Master Xavier's shoulders were slumped just like Marco's. Olivia tried to take his hand, but he shook her off.

Bianca turned back to look at Marco. He met her eyes and shrugged. 'Useless. I'll have to leave the troupe.'

'I'll help you get over it, I promise!'

'How?' Marco asked bitterly.

'Well, I don't know yet, but I'll figure it out, I've got to.'

'Why do you care?' Marco asked, sounding like a sulky kid.

'Because I'm feeling so rubbish at everything else, being a good friend is *something* I should be able to do.'

She plopped herself down next to Marco.

'What's going on?' he asked, his voice softening.

'You know Master di Lombardi's will was read yesterday,' Bianca told him. 'Duchess Catriona gave me his studio to run.'

Marco's mouth made a silent 'O'.

'And I don't think I can do it,' Bianca blurted out. 'I might've been our master's secret favourite or something but I haven't got the first clue how to actually do what he did! And Cosimo and Lucia know it, and they're being horrible. So even if I *could* have managed I won't while they're around. Now our first commission is going to be late – and probably all the rest too, unless I quit.' She looked up and shrugged at Marco's stunned expression.

'Wow,' said Marco. 'I had no idea. Sorry.'

Bianca reached into her pocket. 'And there's more. Master di Lombardi left me a letter.' She unfolded the letter and showed Marco its nonsensical, blurry squiggles. 'A letter I can't read! How's that for useless?' She leaned against the furnace and stared at the letter, unfocusing and crossing her eyes, but it was no good – the writing still didn't make any sense.

'Wait!' Marco said, springing to his feet. 'Hold still! Freeze!'

'What?'

Marco grabbed her hands and held them still. He squinted over her shoulder.

'To make a . . . *storia* . . . take one bottle of *lux aurumque*,' he said slowly. 'Add a spoonful of *animare* to a fifty/fifty mixture of water and *ether* . . .'

'What?' Bianca spun around and found herself face to face with herself. Or rather, her reflection in the dressing-room mirror.

'It's written backwards!' Marco took the letter and turned it so the writing reflected in the mirror. Bianca stared, her mouth dropping open in amazement, as the unreadable scrawl turned into a blurry but readable list of ingredients.

'It's a recipe!' she gasped. 'But why? Why would Master di Lombardi leave me a paint recipe?' At first she felt a little disappointed – she was half-expecting some kind of message. But as she and Marco stood and read the letter together, her stomach twisted with excitement – she'd never seen this recipe before. Or anything like it.

To make a storia, the letter read, *take one bottle of* lux aurumque *and add a spoonful of* animare *to a fifty/fifty mixture of water and* ether. *Drop in a single one of your hairs and wait until it has completely disappeared. Add two crushed, fermented Indigofera leaves, a single flake of gold leaf and two hairs from a black cat. Mix with crushed bone until the paint takes on the texture of thin cream.*

Speak the words: mio cario, narrare storia.

Paint the storia *onto a plain canvas.*

'You have to try and make it,' Marco said. 'Have you got all the ingredients?'

Bianca nodded. 'I think they're all in Filpepi's storeroom . . . everything except my hair and the hair of a black cat. It's very odd, I've never used hair in a paint recipe before. I didn't know you could. And I don't know where I'm going to find a black cat that'll let me pull its hair out!' she added.

'Oh, that's easy!' Marco grinned. 'The master blacksmith has a fat black cat called Nimbus. She's like a friendly, furry sack of potatoes! I'll grab a couple of her hairs and meet you at the palace tomorrow.'

'Are you sure?'

Marco shrugged. 'You said you'd try and help me. It's the least I can do to help you. Anyway,' he added, his face falling, 'I don't think anyone's going to miss me too much if I'm not in the show tomorrow.'

Bianca gave him a sideways smile. 'All right. Thanks! I'll meet you in the courtyard at sunset tomorrow and we can try it out then. I suppose I'll have to be working in the studio all day.'

The two of them sighed heavily at each other, and then Bianca caught Marco's doleful eyes and they both cracked up.

'Do you feel like you've aged about twenty years in the last two months?' Bianca giggled.

Marco snorted. 'Make that a hundred!'

'We'll work it out,' she said. 'Both of us. I promise.'

Chapter Eight

'Mistress Bianca?'

'Hmm?' Bianca rolled over in bed and yawned.

'Mistress Bianca, the Duchess requires your urgent attendance in the throne room,' said the maid, bobbing a low curtsey.

Bianca sat up, suddenly wide awake. 'Erm, yes! Coming!' She half-fell out of bed and let the maid pour her into a blue court dress, her mind in a whirl as she tied the medallion around her neck and tucked it away inside her bodice. What was it? Had something happened to Marco, or one of the apprentices? Or could it be something good – had the Baron and Filpepi been caught and arrested?

She tried not to wear herself out with guessing as she hurried to the throne room, her thin court shoes slapping an uneven rhythm on the tiled floor.

'Mistress Bianca, Court Artist-In-Residence!' announced the footman, opening the throne room doors. Bianca tried to catch her breath as she walked inside. The throne room was lined with courtiers, and every one turned to watch her as she approached the throne.

Duchess Catriona was sitting with her chin resting on one hand, picking at the lace on her ruby red skirt with the other. She looked at Bianca from under furrowed eyebrows. That wasn't a good sign.

'You called for me, Duchess?' Bianca asked.

'Yes, *Mistress* Bianca,' said Duchess Catriona. 'I did.'

The sarcasm in the Duchess's voice stopped Bianca in her tracks. *Oh no, not you too!*

'I've been hearing some disappointing things,' the Duchess said, sitting up and leaning forward. 'Things I don't want to believe . . .'

Bianca took a deep breath and knelt before the throne. She could feel the gazes of the courtiers on the back of her neck. She hoped this would be over quickly so that Catriona could give the studio to Cosimo and they could all get on with their lives.

'Your apprentices tell me that you arrived late yesterday and vanished after only a few hours. Is this true?'

'Yes, Your Highness,' Bianca said. 'But . . .' She tried to think of a way to say *But they were all being horrible to me* without sounding childish.

Duchess Catriona shook her head. 'I didn't put you in charge of the studios so you could throw your weight around! I put you there to work! Your apprentices also tell me that all of the open commissions will be at least a week late. How do you answer that?'

'I . . . I don't know, Your Highness,' Bianca mumbled. She could tell that her face was turning bright red and briefly felt a stab of anger. Why couldn't they have had this conversation in private?

'Don't know?' the Duchess snapped. 'It's your job to know!'

'Yes.' Bianca cringed. 'But the Cathedral commission –'

'Yes, and what explanation do you have for that?' Duchess Catriona asked. 'That painting was your responsibility. Archbishop di Sarvos!' She summoned the old priest over to the throne with a snap of her fingers. Bianca looked up into his sternly wrinkled face and swallowed. 'Bianca, tell the Archbishop just how you're going to make sure his painting is found.'

'I . . . *found*?'

'Yes. The painting went missing on its way to the Cathedral. Whether it's lost or stolen or fallen into the canal, nobody seems to know.'

Bianca wracked her brain. How could it have gone missing? Surely it wasn't even finished? Or had the apprentices worked on it all day, only for it to vanish? 'I'll find out who saw it last,' she said, 'and, and . . .' Inspiration struck. 'And if I can't find it, I'll have the studio make a new one – better than the last, more magical, at no extra cost to the Church,' she said. 'I promise.'

'All right. Thank you, di Sarvos,' said Duchess Catriona, dismissing the priest with a wave of her hand before he even had a chance to respond to Bianca's offer. 'Stand up, Bianca.'

Bianca clambered quickly to her feet and bowed to the Duchess.

Duchess Catriona sat back in her throne. 'I don't mean to be harsh,' she said. 'I know what it's like to have to deal with a huge responsibility when you'd rather be off with your friends,' she added, meeting Bianca's eyes and flashing her a lopsided smile. Then her face turned serious again. 'I know I could have picked one of the older apprentices, or Carlo de Seville or Laura Dexteris – her reputation especially is growing by the day. But I didn't, Bianca. I chose you. And I want you to fix this. For the sake of Master di Lombardi's legacy.'

'I will,' Bianca said, and she meant it. The Duchess was right – she needed to do better.

'OK then, shoo,' said Duchess Catriona, and she threw her a wink.

Bianca set off at once for the studio, hurrying through the secret passages to the painting in Filpepi's office so that she would be there before any of the apprentices arrived. She'd half-hoped that the Duchess was mistaken, that the Cathedral's painting would be on its easel where she'd left it. But it was gone. Bianca spent a few minutes tidying up the paperwork, which she wasn't even surprised to see had been scattered across the floor, and then sat down to wait.

The apprentices all arrived together. Bianca could hear Lucia giving them orders as they came down the corridor. She tried not to feel annoyed – she had walked out on them yesterday, after all. Lucia was just being a good head apprentice. Then Bianca heard her own name and stiffened.

'. . . wouldn't be surprised if she doesn't even show – Oh.' Lucia stopped, her jaw dropping when she saw Bianca sitting in the studio.

'Good morning,' said Bianca coolly.

'Morning, Mistress Bianca,' Gabriella chanted in a childish

sing-song voice. Bianca put down the papers she'd been reading and tried to give them all a stern look.

'I need to know what happened to the Cathedral painting. Who saw it last?'

The younger apprentices all looked around with expressions of perfect innocence, which was pretty suspicious, but not as suspicious as Rosa, Ezio, Cosimo and Lucia's nonchalant silence.

'Rosa, did you finish it?'

'We all worked on it together,' said Rosa. 'After you left. We worked all night.'

Bianca nodded. 'And who packed it up to be transported?'

'I did,' said Lucia.

'And who handed it over to the courier?'

There was silence again. Bianca waited as long as she could bring herself to, hoping the uncomfortable pause would get one of the others to speak – but it was no good. Each apprentice looked as clueless as the next.

'So we don't know whether they actually picked it up? Or who let them in? So it could have been lost, or stolen, or anything? And you have no idea what happened?'

'I bet it was stolen,' said Gabriella.

Lucia nodded. 'I should think so,' she said. 'I know if I was Laura Dexteris . . .' Lucia paused and put her hand to her mouth dramatically as if she had said too much.

Bianca couldn't believe Lucia was blaming Laura Dexteris – an artist from the south of the city whose detailed religious frescoes were earning her a growing reputation and increasingly valuable commissions. It just didn't make sense that she would *steal* another artist's painting. Bianca addressed the bowed figure of Lucia with gritted teeth. 'Please . . . go on, Lucia.'

Lucia looked up at Bianca with a cool gaze. 'If I was Laura Dexteris I'd want to make sure the di Lombardi name was ruined. The name is all we have, after all.'

'That's not true,' said Bianca. 'I know Master di Lombardi has gone, but you're all wonderful artists. And di Lombardi and Filpepi's secrets are still safe with us – with me. We'd be in a perfectly good position if . . .' She swallowed back the words *if you'd all just stop fighting me at every step*. 'If we could just catch up on the schedule.'

'You really are in your own little world, aren't you?' Lucia sneered. 'Face it, girl. None of us would be here if we didn't owe the Duchess a debt for not throwing us all in jail when Filpepi betrayed her. Cosimo and I could've set up our own studios. The rest would've found work with other artists. But no – we stayed here, to be bossed around by an incompetent *child*.'

The blood rushed to Bianca's cheeks. She got up from her chair and stood in front of her apprentices. 'I might not be the best master ever but I'd be a lot better if you weren't such a bully!' she snapped.

'What, do you think the Duchess gave you this position because of your talent? Because of your experience?' Lucia's hand snaked out and she snatched di Lombardi's letter out of Bianca's pocket. She held it up to the other apprentices. 'This is the only reason you're even here – because you were di Lombardi's pet. It's not going to help you find the

Archbishop's painting, is it?'

'Give that back!' Bianca shouted. She made a grab for the paper and it crumpled in her hand as she tugged it out of Lucia's grip. She folded it carefully and shoved it in her pocket. 'It was you, wasn't it? You snuck down here last night, or this morning, and got rid of the painting somehow!'

Lucia crossed her arms. 'I didn't. And I can prove it. Can't I, Cosimo?'

Bianca planted her hands on her hips, feeling more than a bit ridiculous as she looked up into Cosimo's face. He looked uncomfortable, his face flushed, and then he met Lucia's eyes and nodded.

'Yes. Lucia didn't come down here last night. She was, um . . . she was with me. All night.'

Gabriella and Gennaro burst out into giggles, and Rosa's cheeks darkened as she stared at the ceiling.

Yuck! Bianca met Cosimo's eyes, and her shoulders slumped. He might be bossy and annoying and way too susceptible to Lucia's bad influence, but she knew he wouldn't lie to her. Anyway, who in their right mind would say they were Lucia's boyfriend if it wasn't true?

'Fine,' she said. 'But there's still a rule, you know! Apprentices need to concentrate on their work, *not* their fellow apprentices!'

Lucia gave a short laugh. 'That's a stupid rule. Are you going to fire us, girl? I'm trembling, *honestly*.'

Bianca ground her teeth together. She knew she couldn't get rid of Lucia without also firing Cosimo, and anyway she couldn't afford to lose either of them. *I'm not going to give her the satisfaction.*

'No, I am not going to fire you. You're going to help me redo the Archbishop's commission,' she said. 'All of you. I don't think there's much chance of finding it, so we're going to work on it in sections until it's done.' All the apprentices groaned, but Bianca held up her hands. 'It'll go quicker if we all do some. I won't slack off, either. It'll be done in no time – I promise.'

There was a general shrugging and muttering, but at least none of them seemed to actually be about to mutiny. Cosimo even helped Bianca to stretch the canvas over a new frame without being asked.

She couldn't help sneaking a look at him as they worked. She knew he was basically an adult now, old enough to marry Lucia if he'd really wanted to – though the idea gave her the creeping chills. But she still kind of wanted to ask him *why* – for the love of paint, why *Lucia*? She was a bully, and she wasn't even as good an artist as him! But she managed to control herself, deciding to focus on her work.

As the morning wore on, Bianca allowed herself to hope that the pressure was actually going to be good for them all in the end. Francesca and Sebastiano worked well together on the background washes for the sweeping hills and little dips of the golden valley, carefully copying di Lombardi's original sketches for the layout, and they seemed pleased when Bianca told them they were doing good work. Gabriella took charge of the far left hand of the painting, adding trees and the distant blue of faraway mountains, and even though Bianca didn't think she'd ever *like* her, she did at least seem to want to do the best work she could. With Ezio working on the right and Domenico in the middle, it wasn't long before Rosa and Gennaro were able to begin the pilgrims, and Rosa took Bianca's suggestion of repositioning the white-robed priest without complaint.

Bianca herself moved around the canvas, focusing on small details, trying to contribute without getting in anyone's way. She painted small white flowers that dotted the grassy hill in the foreground, then climbed up on a stepladder and animated a flock of birds that shot across the sky. Cosimo and Lucia worked around them all with the *ether* and the *shimmer*, adding space and glow to the painting. Even Lucia's work was beautiful – she certainly knew how to make it seem as though the soft golden light was pouring out of the painted sky into the room.

'That's great!' Bianca said, standing back to take in the whole. Then her eyes fell on the rolling hills, and her pretty white flowers . . . and they were gone. They'd been painted over with swaying grass, as if they'd never been there. She looked up at the patch of sky, searching for her birds, but they'd vanished too. Her gaze flashed back and forth over the painting – every change she'd made had been rubbed out or painted over. Even the fat priest was back in his original position.

Bianca turned on Lucia, her nostrils flaring with anger. 'Lucia, I can't believe you! Do you hate me this much? You can't even stand it if I paint a couple of flowers on this picture?'

'I don't know what you mean.' Lucia shrugged. 'Last I saw, Gabriella was working on that section.'

Gabriella sniggered behind her hand. Bianca sucked in a deep breath to yell at her, but then Cosimo laid a hand on her shoulder.

'Bianca, I think you might be a bit too invested in this,' he said.

'What?'

'It's just . . . I know it hurts when your work doesn't make it into the final painting,' he said, 'but it's not the end of the world. It's just Gabriella being silly. It hasn't hurt the painting.'

'If you can't deal with a little insubordination from the youngsters, it doesn't seem like this is going to be a very good job for you,' said Lucia. Bianca took a deep breath, allowing herself to briefly fantasise about dunking Lucia head first into a bucket of really strong paint remover.

'Well, I promised Duchess Catriona I'd try,' she said, and turned away to pick up the teetering pile of paperwork. 'I don't want to make more work for Gabriella, so I'll be over here, trying to make our supply accounts add up.'

She sat at a nearby bench and sighed at the big pile of receipts and invoices and lists and columns of numbers. They meant little to her except she could recognise that all the numbers seemed intimidatingly large. She was going to try and do this job, and do it properly, if only to spite Lucia. But still, there was a small voice in the back of her head that nagged and tugged at her.

She's right. Even if I could do the job, they'll never let me do it properly.

Maybe it was best for everyone if she gave up trying.

Chapter Nine

'Did you get the cat hairs?'

Marco was waiting in the palace courtyard when Bianca arrived with the last purple rays of the setting sun. He held up a small leather pouch. 'I've got about twenty!'

Bianca shifted the leather bag on her shoulder, and the ingredients inside clinked in their pots. 'And I've got the rest. Come on, let's use my studio in the palace. I don't want to take this to Filpepi's house.'

Marco raised his eyebrows, but he didn't say anything until they'd passed the guards at the door and the lamplighters working on the glowing golden orbs that hung in the halls. When they'd climbed the wide stone steps and turned into the long corridor to the courtiers' apartments, Marco spoke. 'Don't you trust them? Filpepi's apprentices? Do you think they're still working for him?'

'I almost wish I did! No. I'm pretty sure they're not traitors.' Bianca sighed. 'They just hate me.'

Marco furrowed his brow and raised his hands as if about to protest.

'It's OK, I can deal with it,' she said, with a lot more

confidence than she felt. 'But I'm not leaving anything of mine there for them to mess with.' She put a hand up to her neck and twisted a finger under the bright blue string that held the obsidian medallion, tucked securely under her bodice.

Marco blew out a heavy breath between his teeth. 'I dunno. I think I'd still swap with you. I'd rather be hated than pitied.'

Bianca winced as she let them into her rooms. 'That bad?'

'Father can barely look at me. He keeps saying he wishes he knew how to help me get over it. Because *that's* helpful,' he added, rolling his eyes.

'Well, I'll think of something. But right now, let's make a *storia*!' she said, tugging one of her hairs out at the root and holding it up with a flourish.

'Whatever that is,' Marco added with a grin.

Bianca lit all the lamps around the room until the shadows were chased into the corners, then pulled di Lombardi's letter out of her pocket and unfolded it carefully. 'Ugh!' she groaned. 'Lucia's torn it!' *Or maybe I did when I grabbed it back*. Either way, it was Lucia's stupid fault.

'It's all right, I think I can still read it,' said Marco. He smoothed down the ragged tear along the middle of the paper and held it up to the silvered mirror on the wall.

'Read it out to me,' said Bianca, pulling a large ceramic bowl down from a shelf and setting out a steel spoon and an iron stirring stick.

'One bottle of *lux aurumque*,' said Marco. Bianca fished in her bag and pulled out the bottle.

'I hope we get this right,' she muttered, as she uncorked it and let the thick, glowing golden liquid meander its way out into the bowl. 'I'd never normally use a whole bottle! I don't know how much more of this we've got, and all I know is it's made from some kind of flower . . .'

Bianca caught her breath, wondering how she hadn't realised before. The glowing golden flowers! The ones that grew in the gardens and around the statue of di Lombardi in Oscurita!

There *had* to be a way back to Oscurita. How else would di Lombardi and Filpepi have been able to keep making their magical paintings? They had to get fresh ingredients from somewhere . . .

'Bianca? Are you all right?' Marco said. Bianca blinked.

'Fine.' She tried to think how to explain Oscurita to Marco without sounding like she'd gone a bit mad, but he gestured at the *lux aurumque*.

'Only, your paint looks like it's trying to climb out of the bowl.'

'Oh!' Bianca picked up the iron stirrer and tapped gently on the ceramic to make the swirling, shifting *lux aurumque* settle back in the bottom of the bowl. 'Thanks. What's next?'

'Add a spoonful of ani . . . ani . . .'

'*Animare*,' said Bianca, pulling the last of the batch out of the bag.

'. . . to a mixture of fifty/fifty water and *ether*, and then add to the *lux*.'

'Oh, hang on, I need another bowl.' Bianca grabbed a second bowl and carefully measured out the *ether* and the water. They glittered and steamed as they mixed together. She caught Marco staring with wide, fascinated eyes.

'This is so weird,' he said. 'This is like sorcery or something!'

'Well, it basically *is* sorcery,' Bianca admitted, with a smile. She'd forgotten just how magical it all looked when you hadn't seen it done before. 'It's just that we use it to make paint.' She fished in a drawer and handed him a pair of shaded goggles. 'Here, put these on. We don't know what's going to happen when we mix all this stuff together!'

She carefully picked up the single long, brown hair and lowered it slowly into the bowl.

At once, the mixture stopped bubbling and settled. The hair lay on the surface for a second, then fizzed and melted away. Without Bianca even stirring it, the paint turned a glassy silver colour like a mirror, its surface more flat and perfectly reflective than the actual mirror on the wall. Bianca leaned over it and gazed into her own face.

'What now?' she asked Marco.

'Two crushed, fermented Indigofera leaves.'

Bianca used a pair of tweezers to remove the flower petals from the smelly purple liquid they'd been pickling in. 'I guess this is for colour,' she told Marco as she dropped them into a mortar and ground them up quickly. 'These are just normal ingredients. We use them for making indigo paint.'

She scraped the crushed leaves into the mixture and stirred it up with the iron stick – and yes, it slowly turned a deep, metallic blue colour.

'And a single flake of gold leaf,' Marco went on.

Bianca very carefully removed the silk covering from a sheet of gold that'd been pounded so thin it was like a piece of tissue. The corner flaked off at the lightest touch of her tweezers and she held her breath so it wouldn't blow away before she could drop it in the mixture.

'And now, Nimbus's contribution,' Marco said, holding out the small bag. Bianca reached inside and carefully separated two of the short black hairs from the clump that clung to the sides of the bag.

She dropped the hairs in, and they fizzed and melted into the paint just like her own hair had, but instead of silver, the mixture instantly turned a deep, glistening blue-black with strange highlights of green and purple, just like the shell of a beetle. Or like the surface of the obsidian medallion.

'Now just add some ground bone for texture,' Bianca muttered, carefully stirring in a few spoonfuls of the grainy white substance. 'And then speak the words . . .' She peered over Marco's shoulder and he held up the letter to the mirror so she could read them. 'Argh,' she muttered, 'they're right on the tear!'

She pulled the torn halves of the paper together, held it up to the mirror and squinted at the words:

'Mio cario, narrare storia.'

The paint didn't change. Marco leaned over and peered into the bowl. 'Did it work?'

'Only one way to find out,' Bianca said. She lifted a fresh canvas onto the easel, pulled out di Lombardi's magical paintbrush and carefully dipped it into the paint. Then she hesitated. 'But what should I paint?'

92

'How about me?' Marco suggested, striking a heroic pose with his nose in the air. Bianca laughed and put her paintbrush to the canvas, drawing it across and up in a sweeping line that would form the dramatic turn of Marco's chin.

'Hey!' Bianca almost dropped the paintbrush in shock. The paint was moving by itself! It crawled up the canvas, into the top left hand corner, and formed itself into a group of thin vertical lines.

'Wow . . .' Marco dropped the pose. 'What's it doing?'

'I don't know!' Bianca tried again, painting a circle in the centre of the canvas – but again the paint crawled away, like raindrops running down glass but in reverse, to join the picture that was forming in the corner of the canvas. 'It . . . it doesn't want to stay where I put it. It's like it has a painting already stored inside itself!'

'Amazing!' Marco peered at the picture as the paint settled. 'It looks like a street and a canal, but there's something weird about it. All the buildings are black.'

'Oh,' Bianca breathed. Was this it? Could it be? 'Oscurita!'

'Huh?' Marco asked.

Bianca quickly added several more large brushfuls of paint. The picture filled out. It was definitely a picture of a street in Oscurita. The areas of canvas where the paint left gaps shone out as bright lights and patches of reflection on the canal.

'I need to tell you something,' said Bianca, as she hurried to add more paint, the picture growing until it almost filled the canvas. 'Remember when Filpepi and the Baron escaped into that painted trapdoor? Did you see what was on the other side?'

'It just looked dark to me,' Marco shrugged.

'It was a city, just like this one, except there's no sunlight, and everyone wears black. I think I've been sleepwalking there.'

'What? How?'

'I don't know. At first I thought I was dreaming. But the other night I actually brought something back with me. Look!' Bianca fished in her pocket and pulled out the tiny silver bracelet with its pattern of twining flowers.

'This is weird,' Marco muttered, turning the bracelet round in his hands. 'I mean, even compared to your life normally, this is pretty weird!'

'That's all of it,' Bianca said, running her paintbrush along the bottom of the bowl and touching the last drop of paint to the canvas. 'I bet this is a way through to – Oh!' She gasped as all the paint moved once more, running and swirling together and then splitting to form another picture. This time the street was pocked with holes and full of swirling smoke. 'Maybe not,' she said. As they watched, a glob of paint arced across the picture and hit one of the buildings. A chunk of painted masonry crumbled and fell into the canal.

'It's under attack!' Marco breathed.

'Look!' Bianca pointed as the swirling lines of smoke parted and a shape ran through. It was a woman, her skirt and her long dark hair rippling as she sprinted along the street. Bianca just had time to notice that she was clutching a small bundle in her arms, before she ducked into a doorway and the whole painting swirled away again, splitting and re-forming into a scene in a courtyard. A man, wrapped in a dark cloak, turned as the woman ran in. His beard was shorter and his face less wrinkled, but Bianca still recognised him – it was Annunzio di Lombardi.

'Isn't that –' Marco pointed.

Bianca nodded.

The woman and di Lombardi ran to each other and he put his hands on her face and kissed her forehead. Tears ran down the woman's cheeks.

Bianca recognised the woman. It wasn't quite like looking into a mirror – it was more like when Duchess Catriona stood next to the portraits of her mother.

The woman put her bundle into di Lombardi's arms and he peeled back a flap of blanket. The paint wriggled on the canvas: a squiggle of a mouth that opened into an O and closed again, two fringed lines for closed, thickly eyelashed eyes. Bianca could almost hear the baby's squalling. Di Lombardi pulled the blanket back and looked up at the woman. The paint shimmered, giving hints of colour to the picture – the deep purple of di Lombardi's cloak, the green ribbon that edged the baby's blanket, the woman's blue eyes, just like Bianca's.

Then something weird happened – half the picture seemed to lose its power. The paint dripped lifelessly down the page on the right hand side, while the other half kept swirling and moving as di Lombardi took a step back and held up an object . . .

'My medallion!' Bianca gasped. A flash of light seemed to

burst from its surface. The dead half of the painting sprang back to life just in time to show shadowy figures recoil from the light of the medallion.

'What was that?' Marco wondered.

'Maybe we got the mixture wrong,' Bianca muttered. She pulled out the medallion, which she'd been wearing hidden under her dress, and clutched it until her knuckles went white.

On the canvas, the paint was still telling its story. It showed di Lombardi stepping out into the bright daylight of La Luminosa; sweeping a low bow to someone who must be the Duke, Catriona's father; settling the baby down in a crib beside him as he worked at an easel. Years seemed to pass in a moment: sketchy visions of his masterpieces came and went on the easel. A young man studied at his side.

'That must be Filpepi!' Bianca gasped.

The crib vanished. Patches of the picture froze a couple of times, but the passage of time was clear enough: the baby grew into a toddler, chewing on a paintbrush, and then a little girl with paint on her face. Di Lombardi's beard grew and his back hunched. The apprentices appeared – first as young children, then growing quickly until Cosimo and Rosa were as tall as di Lombardi himself. The girl who had been the baby turned and looked straight out of the painting.

It was unmistakably Bianca.

'You didn't know any of this?' Marco asked.

'He told me I was a foundling someone left on his doorstep!' Bianca said. She looked down at the medallion. 'You realise what this means? I'm not from here at all . . .

I was born in Oscurita!'

'That woman has to be your mother,' Marco said.

'I think so,' whispered Bianca.

The story hadn't finished. Bianca's eyes prickled with tears as she realised that the painting of her was growing older. They were looking at a version of the future, as di Lombardi had imagined it. He'd painted himself, alive, alongside her as she grew up. The painting showed the now-adult Bianca and di Lombardi embracing, and then she walked away. Then the scene switched back to Oscurita, the paint flooding back to the top of the canvas to show the black sky. The painted Bianca walked through the front gates of the castle and up to one of the twisting circular towers . . .

The painting froze. The paint that'd made the sky dark streamed down the canvas, blocking out any movement that might've been going on underneath. Bianca made a frustrated noise in the back of her throat. But then the painting was back, only a second later, and it showed the secret passages. The black door swung open, and the woman who must be Bianca's mother, now middle-aged, stepped through. She and Bianca embraced.

Then the scene split apart and snaking lines spun across the canvas. It wasn't a picture of anything Bianca could make out at first. Then symbols started to pop up: a church cross, a crown, a little house . . .

'It's a map!' Marco said, as the paint slowed and finally stopped moving altogether. They both held their breath in case there was more to the story, but nothing else happened.

'It must be a map of Oscurita.' Bianca reached up and

gingerly touched a finger to one of the lines. The paint was perfectly dry. She fished in a drawer for a knife and carefully cut the canvas out of its frame. Marco took it over to a table and peered down at it, frowning at the strange pattern of criss-crossing streets.

'It's a weird shape for a city,' he muttered.

'It's a weird city,' Bianca said. 'But I've always felt at home there. And now I know why! I have to get back.'

Marco looked up. '*This* is your home, though,' he said. 'You grew up in La Luminosa – all your friends are here, your studio, your whole life. Are you sure you want to go back to this place just because you happen to have been born there?'

'Of course! My mother is still alive, I'm sure I saw her last time I was sleepwalking. I think – this is going to sound mad, Marco . . . but I think my mother is the Duchess of Oscurita.'

Marco raised a sceptical eyebrow. 'The Duchess. Really.'

'It doesn't sound very likely, does it?' Bianca glanced at her reflection in the mirror. 'I've always been basically nobody. No mother or father, no history, nothing that was *mine* except what Master di Lombardi gave me.' She touched the medallion again. It gleamed darkly under her fingers. 'But everyone's got to be *someone,* haven't they?'

'You are someone,' Marco said. 'You're you!'

'But why did my mother give me to Master di Lombardi in the first place? What was so terrible in Oscurita that she had to give me up?' said Bianca.

'Di Lombardi must've had his reasons for keeping all

this a secret. You were an adult when you went back in di Lombardi's version. He obviously meant for you to wait.'

'He meant to be alive, too,' Bianca said.

An uncomfortable silence filled the room and Bianca's hand strayed to the paintbrush. She hadn't cleaned it, and cleaning brushes as quickly as possible was something you learned on day one of being an apprentice. She hurried over to the small porcelain sink and rinsed the bristles carefully with a dash of paint remover and some water from a copper jug.

'Anyway, Duchess or not, my mother needs help,' said Bianca. 'If everything I saw in my dreams is as real as this bracelet, the Baron da Russo did find his way into Oscurita, and my mother's been talking to him. He's probably planning to betray her just like he did Catriona! What if he kills her?'

'Or worse, tries to marry her?' Marco pointed out.

Bianca shuddered. 'I've got to get back and save her before something awful happens!'

'But how are you going to get there? You said you didn't know the way.'

Bianca's heart sank. 'I don't know,' she said quietly. She'd looked for the door all over the secret passages, and she'd tried painting her own way through. All without success.

She carefully dried the paintbrush on a scrap of cotton and turned to lean on the sink, her shoulders sagging.

'All right,' said Marco. '*If* you don't forget your promise and help me get over my thing about heights, I'll help you find a way into this dark city from your dreams . . . even though it's obviously mad. Deal?'

Bianca grabbed him into a fierce hug. 'You are the best.'
She smiled down at the mysterious map.
I'm coming, Mother. I'll find a way.

Chapter Ten

'Mistress Bianca!'

Bianca looked up from the map and hurriedly dropped into a curtsey. 'Your Highness!'

Duchess Catriona stood in the doorway, her hands planted on her hips. Behind her, Secretary Franco and Archbishop di Sarvos loomed, glaring at Bianca as if she was a street urchin who'd been caught sitting on the throne. Their glares were so alike they could've been brothers, except that Franco was thin and hunched like a vulture and di Sarvos was tall and solid, as if someone had put a red and white robe on a tree trunk. The top of his pointy hat nearly brushed the door frame.

'Mistress Bianca, *a moment of your time*,' Duchess Catriona said, packing so much haughty chill into those words that Bianca shuddered.

'I'll just . . .' Marco quickly rolled up the map of Oscurita and shrugged towards the door. 'Excuse me, Your Highness, your worship, Secretary Franco.' He bobbed a bow to each of them and squeezed past, turning back at the last second to gesture to the map and give Bianca a thumbs up. Bianca nodded back, but she couldn't manage a smile.

'Mistress Bianca, what are you doing here?' Duchess Catriona demanded.

Bianca blinked, confused. 'Um . . . it's long past sunset, Your Majesty.'

'Do you think the Duchess is blind, child?' snapped Secretary Franco, gesturing to the open window, where the deep blue-black sky was full of glittering stars.

'No.' Bianca met Duchess Catriona's eyes, hoping for understanding, but Catriona's expression remained stony. 'I'm sorry, Your Highness,' she said, bobbing a curtsey. 'I only meant that the studio is closed.'

'I'm aware,' said the Duchess. 'But why are you *here*, Bianca? And *where* is Archbishop di Sarvos's commissioned painting?'

'Oh.'

'Yes, *oh*!' barked the Archbishop. 'You swore before the Duchess you were going to do everything you could to find it!'

'Instead,' Duchess Catriona continued for him, 'I hear you went back to the studio and asked your apprentices to begin a new painting, and haven't made any other enquiries!'

Lucia, Bianca thought.

She curtseyed again to mask her annoyance and gather her thoughts. 'I did make enquiries, Your Highness. I found out that the painting was finished on time and left in the studio. Unfortunately, none of the apprentices made sure they were there when it was picked up, and it . . . it just vanished. So I just thought –'

'You thought you wouldn't even try?' sneered Secretary Franco.

The rest of Bianca's careful patience drained away. 'Your Highness, your worship, with all due respect,' she said, 'I thought there was no point chasing it all over the city with no clues to go on. I made the decision to have the painting redone. It will be quicker!'

'And then you left it to your apprentices!'

Because they drove me away! Shame rose in Bianca's throat, choking her.

No, that's not good enough. I let myself be driven away.

Deep down, she knew this was ridiculous. They were only *her* apprentices through chance, and Cosimo and Rosa – and yes, Lucia – were just as good as she was. But that wasn't enough. She was the mistress of the studio now, and they were her responsibility.

'I . . . I supervised them for most of the day. But the painting was in good hands, and if I didn't do some of the paperwork there wouldn't be any more paint for the next commission!'

'Excuses!' Duchess Catriona snapped. She raised her voice and her face flushed deep pink, clashing horribly with the golden-red glow of her freckles and her hair. 'This painting for Archbishop di Sarvos is the most important commission the studio has had for years, and I won't have you cutting corners! It's as if you don't care what happens to Master di Lombardi's legacy.'

Don't care? Bianca bit hard on her lip and looked out of the window, desperately hoping the two looming courtiers

103

wouldn't see the tears springing into her eyes. But it didn't help – the glittering stars blurred together like a painting that'd been left out in the rain. *How . . . how could she say that?*

Duchess Catriona sighed. 'Get out, you two. I want to speak to my Master Artist alone.'

Bianca risked a glance at the two men. They stayed where they were until Duchess Catriona spun on her heel and fixed them with the same angry glare she'd been giving Bianca.

'Out! Don't make me scream for Captain Raphaeli!'

The Secretary and the Archbishop glanced at each other, bowed quickly and ducked out of the room. Bianca found herself smiling through her tears. Nobody would've wanted to be on the bad side of the Duchess if the Captain of the Guard heard her scream . . . he might run them through with his spear first and ask questions later.

'Poor Captain Raphaeli,' said Duchess Catriona, watching the two men scarper. 'He blames himself terribly for the traitors' escape, and I repay him by using him as my personal bogeyman.'

She turned to Bianca, who wiped her eyes hurriedly and braced herself for another bout of shouting. But Duchess Catriona's face had softened. She walked around the table to Bianca's side and took her hand.

'Dear Bianca. You know, it's not actually about the commission.'

'It . . . it's not?'

'God, no. I'm sure however you want to handle it is perfectly fine. I'm sorry I had to shout at you – it was only because old di Sarvos wouldn't shut up about it. He's been going on at me all day. I swear, if he so much as mentions it after this I've half a mind to put his head on a spike outside the throne room!'

Bianca gave a sniffly giggle. 'You wouldn't!' she said.

Duchess Catriona laughed. 'Oh, Bianca, nobody's had their head put on a spike since my Great-Great-Grandmother Regina's day; I'm not going to be the one to bring it back!' She squeezed Bianca's hand again. 'But I really am concerned.'

The tears rose again.

'Me too,' she admitted.

'Let me show you something, Bianca.' Duchess Catriona crossed Bianca's bedroom. Bianca followed, rubbing her eyes and trying to pull herself together.

The Duchess pulled the door to Bianca's balcony open and stepped outside. Bianca shuddered as the cool evening breeze mingled on her skin with the heat radiating from the pale stones of the palace walls. The Duchess leaned on the carved wooden balcony and looked down into the city.

'Look there,' she said, pointing down into a square just on the other side of the Grand Canal.

Bianca looked. She recognised the building at once – it was the Royal Museum of Art. Coloured banners hung from the windows and the tiles of the courtyard were laid in a beautiful mosaic of a tree with golden leaves growing on its spreading branches. Statues of lions, sculpted by di Lombardi himself, reared up on either side of the door.

But the courtyard was empty. Bianca frowned. Normally the Museum was open late into the night, teeming with visitors who'd come to see La Luminosa's great artworks. But today it looked deserted, and the lights that normally blazed in the windows were dim.

'It's not your fault, Bianca,' Duchess Catriona said. 'It's just that with Master di Lombardi gone and Filpepi proved a traitor, the city has lost two of its greatest artists at once. People don't want to think about those things, so they're staying away from the Museum.'

'They'll come back,' Bianca pointed out.

Duchess Catriona nodded. 'I'm sure they will. But by then, the damage will have been done.' She turned to face Bianca, leaning against the railing. 'I have grand plans, Bianca. I want to give my patronage to scientists and inventors and performers and doctors. I'm going to build colleges and an academy for music.' The Duchess's face took on a dreamy expression as she gazed out over the city. 'I know it won't all happen overnight.' Her voice turned serious. 'But I won't tolerate any backward steps either. I need someone who can be *fully committed* to making the people of this city remember that they live in the greatest artistic city in the world!'

'You shouldn't have chosen me,' Bianca said. 'None of the apprentices will listen to me because they think I can't do it.' Her throat tightened. 'Maybe they're right. I don't have enough experience of managing things. I can paint, but not well enough to be a master!'

'*I* believe in you, Bianca,' Duchess Catriona said. 'Are you saying I'm mistaken?'

'Yes,' Bianca whispered. There was an uncomfortable

106

silence. 'Please don't have my head put on a spike.'

They smiled at each other for a second, then Bianca stared at the floor.

'You *do* need someone who's fully committed.' *And I don't know if my mind is going to be on my work right now,* Bianca thought. *I have to open the way to the dark city and try to find my mother.* 'You should make Cosimo the master of the studios,' she said firmly. 'I'll go back to being an apprentice, and I'll teach him Master di Lombardi's secrets so they won't need to rely on me.'

So they won't miss me.

Duchess Catriona shook her head. 'I don't want to just strip you of your position like this! If they don't like you now, imagine what they'll do if you're demoted,' she pointed out, with a grim smile. She looked down at the Museum again, and her eyes sparkled. 'I know! I'll hold a competition!' She clapped her hands. 'Yes, it'll be great – any artist in the city will be allowed to submit a painting, and the best painting will win control of both studios. That's fair, isn't it?'

'Yes,' Bianca said, smiling. 'That sounds very fair! I'm sure Cosimo and Lucia will both enter, and the best artist will win.' She couldn't help hoping it would be Cosimo.

'But I will only do this if you enter too,' Duchess Catriona said.

'But –' Bianca started. She wasn't good enough – she didn't want to humiliate herself by letting the world find out what she already knew.

'No arguments. That way it'll show them – *and you* – that you're the greatest artist and I was right to choose you all along!' The Duchess nudged her with her elbow. 'I can't have people thinking a duchess could ever make a mistake now, can I?'

Bianca tried not to let her face fall. 'You're too kind to me, Your Highness.'

'Bianca.' Duchess Catriona frowned. 'You saved my life, and my crown. I owe you and Marco and Master di Lombardi everything.' She reached out and squeezed Bianca's hands again. 'If there's any other service I can do, you know you only need to ask. Promise me you will ask!'

Bianca smiled and bobbed half a curtsey. 'I promise.'

Duchess Catriona grinned and threw her arm around Bianca's shoulder. 'Ugh, I tire of all this drama. Let's go and have the master cook make us some honeycakes.'

Bianca's laugh echoed down the palace corridors. It was nice to have a friend who believed in her. And the fact that her friend was actually a duchess made it all the more brilliant. But it also made the idea of failing her all the worse.

Chapter Eleven

Bianca brushed herself down as she stood and walked carefully to the edge of the deep ravine, peering down past its sharp crags to the churning white foam in the rushing river far below. 'I think it's ready,' she said.

'Yeah, I can see that,' said Marco, peering through his fingers.

Bianca regarded the patch of her bedroom floor where she'd painted the ravine. It was about two metres wide, running almost all the way across the room at the foot of her bed so it looked as if most of the floor had fallen away.

She'd painted a tightrope strung across it. She picked up the broom she'd borrowed from one of the maids and prodded the rope, which wobbled convincingly. Not bad for a morning's work!

'Let me show you.' Bianca walked around the ravine, grabbed one of Marco's hands and dragged it away from his eyes. With her other hand she dropped the broom into the ravine. It went down into the floor for about half a metre, and then stopped. The rushing waters of the river crashed around it. 'See? It only *looks* very deep. It's a perspective trick! I promise it's safe.'

'You can promise all you like . . .' Marco turned his head away, straining not to look at the painted ravine.

'Look, I said I'd help you – this is the only way I can think of!' Bianca said. 'At least try it.'

Marco sucked in a deep breath though his teeth and turned to face the vast crevasse in front of him. Sweat beaded on his forehead and his face went pale. Bianca jiggled the broom up and down, to show him again that the painting wasn't deep, then pulled it out and handed it to him. Marco grasped it firmly between his hands, just like one of the long white sticks the troupe sometimes used for balance.

'All right. I can do this,' he said, and took a step forward, so the toes of his foot touched the rope. His throat tightened as he swallowed hard.

'Keep talking,' she suggested.

'I used to be able to do this,' Marco croaked. 'I've walked on tightropes in shows, and climbed high sets.'

'Tell me about them!' Bianca edged along the side of the painting as Marco took one hesitant step and then another, wobbling a little and clutching the broom tightly.

'Well . . . I played a pickpocket who was being chased by the Palace Guard,' Marco said. Bianca nodded encouragingly. It was working! He was out on the rope now. As long as he didn't think about the fire, he would be fine. 'And another time I climbed up a wooden tower with . . . with the others.' A drop of sweat fell from Marco's nose and his hands shook.

'What others? Why were you climbing the tower?' Bianca asked. *Come on, you can do it! Just a few more steps!*

110

'It was . . . there was . . . Olivia was playing the Queen of Arcadia, and we . . . we were . . . we were the Knights of . . . nope. Nope. Nope.' He froze and squeezed his eyes shut. 'Sorry, I know you worked on it all morning, but . . . I can't.'

'It's OK, you're doing so well!' Bianca said. 'You're nearly halfway across, you can make it!'

'I can't,' Marco said with a shaky exhalation of breath. 'I can smell smoke. I can't see . . .'

His eyes were still firmly closed, but Bianca guessed that pointing that out to him wouldn't be helpful. She sighed and hopped down into the ravine, so Marco's trembling feet were at waist height. She reached up a hand to take his elbow. 'I'm here. Hold on to me.'

Marco's hands shook as he let go of the broom and groped for her. He missed her outstretched hand and grabbed the top of her head.

'Ow!' Bianca winced as his fingers gripped tightly on to her hair. 'It's all right. Just hold on.'

She walked him carefully forward, holding him steady as his shaking toes felt for a grip on the painted rope. Finally he touched solid ground and stumbled forward onto his hands and knees, gasping.

Bianca hopped up to sit on the edge of the painting, her legs dangling into the magical space. The perspective trick made them look like a giant's legs, ending in feet as wide as the whole ravine.

'Sorry,' she said, as Marco sat back and hurriedly wiped the sweat from his neck with the end of his sleeve. 'Maybe

I should've made it shallower.'

'I'm not sure this is ever going to work,' Marco said miserably.

'Maybe if we just give it time. This is only our first try.'

'Yeah. Maybe.'

They fell silent for a few seconds, then Marco hopped to his feet.

'Now it's my turn.'

Bianca looked up from kicking her heels against the strangely woody-feeling sides of the rocky-looking cliffs. 'Your turn? To do what?'

'To help you!' Marco gave her a broad grin and went over to the bag he'd brought with him. 'I've been looking at the map di Lombardi left you, and I've got a theory. Take this,' he added, holding out a second piece of rolled-up parchment.

Bianca climbed out of the painting and took it from him. She unrolled it. 'A map of La Luminosa,' she said.

'We should go into the studio,' Marco said. 'We need a flat surface, and you made a big hole in this one!' He chuckled as he nodded towards the painting on the floor, but his eyes were still worried.

'Course,' said Bianca, and carried the map of La Luminosa into the studio. Rolling it out on the worktop, she pinned down the curling edges with clean water jars and palette knives.

'OK, so this is La Luminosa. And this is the map di Lombardi painted.' He unrolled the canvas and Bianca helped him pin it onto an easel so they could look at both at the same time. The painted map was on about the same scale, but when she saw it next to the map of La Luminosa, Bianca realised it didn't look much like a map of a city at all. The blue-black lines zigzagged back and forth and criss-crossed the canvas. They formed the vague outline of a city much like La Luminosa, but the streets seemed like they'd been laid out by a frothing madman.

'That's . . . odd,' Bianca frowned at Marco. 'That doesn't look like any city map I've ever seen before.'

'Right?' said Marco. 'When you were in Oscurita – I know you were asleep, but did you notice the streets criss-crossing like this?'

'No, it felt pretty normal.'

Marco stood back and pulled Bianca with him, so she could see both maps laid out in front of her. 'I think it might not be a map of Oscurita after all. See that cluster of lines around where the palace is in La Luminosa?'

Bianca nodded. The detail was incredible, streets narrowing to a single painted line. But *were* they streets? She followed the line on the painted map and the printed one. If you imagined them one on top of the other, it almost looked like the lines were describing a crazy winding path leading around the corridors of the Palace of La Luminosa, visiting different rooms in a seemingly random order before running out into the city again . . .

'Can you see it?' Marco asked. He was practically hopping from foot to foot with glee.

Bianca gasped. 'It's the secret passages!' She leaned in closer, trying to remember the order of the doors. She found Filpepi's studio on the La Luminosa map. Sure enough, a line ran through it on the other map – in fact, there were two! She knew that next to the door into Filpepi's office there was a door to a passage that led to a small chapel, and sure enough the line shot out across La Luminosa and stopped at the nunnery of San Ferdinand.

'This is great!' Bianca clasped her hands in excitement. 'Let's go exploring!'

An hour later, Bianca and Marco sat with their backs propped against the cool paint-spattered walls of the secret passages, exhilarated. The map had worked! They'd been able to find their way from the Rose Gallery painting to the Museum of Art where they'd looked out through the arches in the background of di Lombardi's masterpiece, *The Throne Eternal*. Then they'd simply gone through the next door and been transported across the city to the Via del Orologica in time to see the daily procession of the clockwork monks from their monastery to the Chapel of Chimes.

'This is amazing!' Bianca said, unrolling the map and searching for a location for them to visit next.

'I'll never be late for dinner again,' Marco laughed.

'Where shall we go now?'

Marco leaned forward, examining the spidery trail of lines across the map. 'I fancy having a poke around in one of these grand houses.'

Bianca followed Marco's finger, until something caught her eye on the edge of the map, making her heart pound. 'Wait . . .' she whispered. There was a line that seemed to extend south of the city, past the docks and the mouths of the canals, right into the sea. 'What do you think this means?'

'Maybe it's a painting that was shipwrecked and now it's at the bottom of the sea!' Marco said ghoulishly. 'Maybe we'll be able to look out through a window and see the skeletons of the sailors!'

Bianca was shaking her head in disbelief, barely taking in Marco's words. 'Maybe . . . maybe it means the painting leads to another *place* entirely,' Bianca said quietly.

'Yeah, maybe we'll end up on the Crowfoot Islands! I say we definitely look there next.'

'No, Marco. Don't you see?' Bianca raised her startled face and stared at him, a grin forming on her face. *I think that door opens into somewhere further away than the Crowfoot Islands. Much further.*

Marco raised a questioning eyebrow but stayed silent as Bianca's quivering finger traced the disappearing line backwards all over the city and past about twenty different paintings, until they came to a door they knew.

'I want to go there.' Bianca couldn't keep her voice from quavering with excitement. 'It looks like the best way is to go out through the painting in the Piazza del Oro, cross the canal in the real world and get back in through the mural at the back of the library. Then we just follow the doors to the end.'

Her heart lodged itself in her throat as she quickly rolled up the map and hurried off through the passageways towards the disappearing point shown on the map. Marco followed after her as Bianca glanced through paintings, checking no one was there, before hurtling out the other side. They took a left down a corridor, and were met by a soft bluish glow emanating from the adjacent passageway up ahead. She checked the map to make sure she was where she wanted to be and felt her racing blood pounding in her ears. Round that corner they would be able to see the mysterious doorway.

Bianca counted the steps before she reached the bend, forcing herself to be calm. It was just as likely that the door would lead them to some other country, or the bottom of the sea. She tried to remind herself just how exciting that would be, so she wouldn't be disappointed.

They turned the corner and there, at the end of the corridor, was a black door edged with bright, bright blue.

The door to Oscurita.

'That's the door from my dream!' Bianca clutched the medallion where it lay against her chest. 'We've found Oscurita!'

Marco's mouth dropped wide open, speechless for a moment.

'Now I can explore Oscurita whenever I want,' Bianca said. 'I can find my mother, and warn her about the Baron.'

'Let's go!' Marco stepped towards the door. Bianca hurried forward, and then paused.

'Wait . . .'

Marco turned back. 'What?'

Bianca reached into her dress and pulled out the gleaming medallion.

'I don't think I should bring this with me,' she said. 'It's obviously important, and di Lombardi's message did show me bringing it to Oscurita when I was older. What if the

Baron and Filpepi take it from me? It's much safer here, for now. I'll run back and hide it in my room.'

'Well, hurry up!' Marco complained, sitting down beside the black door and fishing an apple out of his bag. 'I want to see this amazing city.'

Bianca ran back to the palace, hopping out through one painting and in through another, and finally coming back out into the Duke's old sitting room through the mural with the two big cats. She hurried to her bedroom and put the medallion in the pocket of her old painting apron, then wrapped the apron up into a tight ball and put it at the back of the bottom drawer of her dresser.

It ought to be safe there, she thought. As she turned to go, her eye caught the little silver bracelet and she picked it up. *This, I will take with me.* She wasn't sure who it belonged to, after all – she should at least try to return it.

The big cats seemed to turn their emerald and amber eyes on her as she hurried back down the path in the dust – although she knew they were on a normal *animare* cycle and wouldn't take any notice of what she did. She paused to let the tiger cross in front of her and then hopped into the painting and ran her fingers through the lion's mane before letting herself in through the old door.

Marco was standing on one leg and juggling with two apples and an orange when she got back to the black door.

'Getting some practice?' she asked.

'Don't want to get rusty,' said Marco. 'Even if I'm not performing much any more,' he added sadly. 'Come on!'

He stood aside to let Bianca slip the paintbrush key into

the lock. Bianca held her breath. So much could still go wrong – it could be locked, or not really lead to Oscurita after all . . .

The door swung easily open and revealed the abandoned courtyard. A cool breeze touched her face, scented with night jasmine. She'd never *smelled* the city in her dreams, or not that she'd remembered. She took a deep breath and stood back to let Marco look. The darkness almost seemed to spill out into the secret passage.

Marco blinked. 'I can't see anything!'

'It's a courtyard,' said Bianca, pointing. 'Look, there's a flowerbed, and that's an arch. You can see some of the street on the other side.'

Marco peered in through the door, squinting. 'Speak for yourself!'

'Come on.' Bianca stepped down out of the painting and reached back up to help Marco through. 'Your eyes'll adjust soon enough, and there are lights further in.'

'All right . . .' Marco let her help him down and she grinned as he looked around, taking in the black stone and the strange scrubby plants and the flickering from the thunder-lamps out on the street – at least, she assumed he could just about see them. His pupils were so wide his irises had almost disappeared.

Bianca herself took a deep breath of the cool night air and reached out to touch the stone. It felt rough and real.

Finally I'm home.

Chapter Twelve

'Oof!' Marco groaned, stumbling over a crack in the pavement. 'Bianca, how come you can see so well?'

'I'm not sure. Maybe because my parents were from here,' Bianca said, stopping to let him catch up. While Marco focused intently on the space two steps ahead of him, Bianca gazed at the magnificent buildings lining the canals: towers of cobbled black stone and twisting towers, flecked with colour. She ran over the plan she had been devising in her head – if you could call it a *plan*. It was certainly very simple. And risky. But Bianca knew she would do anything it took to find her mother.

They continued walking along a canal street, the black water gurgling gently beside them. Even though she had been here in her dreams, the place definitely felt more real to Bianca now. She could feel the cold air coming up off the canal and smell the oily, wet-wood smells of the boats gliding along its surface.

The city was quiet . . . even tense: why hadn't they come across anyone yet? From the candles in the windows it was clear people lived here. They must be either indoors or congregating somewhere else in the city. *Or maybe they're hiding from something.* Finding her mother might not be as easy as she had thought. Marco said his eyes had adjusted enough for him to mostly see where he was going, but he was clearly still having trouble. He stopped under a thunder-lamp and gazed up at it. 'It's like lightning! But how come it casts so little light?'

'Maybe they make it dimmer so it doesn't melt the glass,' Bianca replied absently. Her eyes darted ahead to a maze of dark alleys: she could see a few figures dressed all in black passing along them now.

Bianca felt herself drawn on, quickening her pace now Marco could keep up. The reflections of the hundreds of candles in the windows of the buildings glittered in the water and onto the streets ahead as if guiding her. She had only been here once before, in her dreams, but it was as if she sensed the way she needed to go, like a powerful force was pulling her towards the castle.

She became aware that Marco was a way behind again and paced back to take his hand. His breaths were ragged and quick and his palms were sweaty.

'It's so quiet,' he said. 'It's like the darkness swallows the sound.'

'I think that's just how it is here,' Bianca replied, pulling him forward onto a narrow bridge. She noticed two men coming towards them from the other side. They were wearing almost matching clothes, except that the linings of their cloaks were different – one bright red, one bright green.

'I wonder why they only wear those little bits of colour?'

Marco whispered.

'Everyone here dresses like that. Why don't people in La Luminosa wear black, apart from priests and doctors?' Bianca said.

Marco shrugged, but then gave her a panicked look. 'Look how we're dressed – it's obvious we're not from this place.'

'Just act normal,' Bianca whispered back.

Marco stared wide-eyed around him. '*Normal?*'

The two men passed by; their conversation cut off as their eyes switched to Bianca and Marco, surveying them with interest. She heard Marco hold his breath . . . but then the men were walking away behind them.

Marco let out a soft whistle. 'They didn't like the look of us. Maybe we sh—'

His words fell away as the black stone figure of di Lombardi rose into the dim sky ahead of them. His eyes flicked from the statue to Bianca and then back again. 'Is that . . . ?'

Bianca grinned. 'Annunzio di Lombardi.'

'He looks so young. He must have been an important artist here too. *Very* important. That stone. It's like black marble or something . . . it's amazing.'

'Just you wait,' said Bianca.

She led them on now, recognising the route from her dream. *We're almost at the castle*, she realised, unable to stop the image of her dramatic return entering her head. It just sounded wrong: Bianca, *Princess* of Oscurita . . .

The market where Bianca had stolen the fruit in her dream came into sight. Marco listed the stalls' exotic wares as if hypnotised: 'Black jewellery, books, birds, furry fruit, some kind of lute.'

Bianca grabbed Marco and turned her face away as she passed two armoured guards – they might still be looking for her.

Exiting the market, she stopped and pointed down a wide avenue, and was gratified to hear Marco's intake of breath as he looked up and saw the Castle of Oscurita.

'We're here,' she told him.

'I can't make out where it ends,' he said. 'It's like it goes all the way up into the clouds!' He squinted at the gate. 'But I can see guards. And they're all holding very pointy sticks. With shiny bits on the end.'

'Spears,' Bianca confirmed. 'And swords.'

'So how're we going to get in and find this Duchess?'

'Just follow my lead,' she said, taking his elbow and pulling him down the avenue, heading for the main bridge over the canal.

Marco groaned. 'If you're not telling me what it is, it can't be good.'

'Trust me.'

'Oh, right. So much better.'

If her plan was to work, she had to act confident. She puffed out her chest and marched them onto the bridge and right up to the guards. They looked down at her from underneath glinting silver helmets that tapered to a point with the same etched swirling patterns on their sides as the guards' breastplates.

'Have you a royal invitation?' one of them grumbled.

'No,' said Bianca. 'But –'

'Pfft.' The guard turned to his companion. 'Urchins.'

'No pass, no entrance to the castle,' said the other guard. 'What're you two selling, eh?'

'Nothing. I'm bringing something back.'

The guard pushed her by the shoulder, firmly turning her around. 'You've tried your luck and failed. Now, go on with you.'

She ducked under him and spun around to face the gates again. 'But I really –' she started, but the guard put his face close up to hers.

'Clear off,' he said. 'You're making me angry!'

'Bianca,' Marco whispered beside her. 'Maybe we should just –'

'No!' she yelled, trying her best to sound like Duchess Catriona. 'I have something for the Duchess and if these two idiots don't take me there this instant . . .' She tailed off as she realised she had no threat to back it up.

The guards thrust their spears forward, the sharp blades digging into the flesh on her neck. 'I'm warning you,' one of them said. 'No one will miss a pair of street rats if we decide to throw you both in the canal.'

Marco backed off but Bianca remained where she was, ignoring the pressure of the spear against her skin. She said nothing as she reached into her pocket and pulled out the silver bracelet, holding it up so it shone in the light from the thunder-lamps.

The first guard glared at them. 'Do you think you can bribe us with that piece of tat?'

But the second guard elbowed him in the breastplate with a clatter. 'That belongs to the Duchess! It was stolen by some raggedy girl a few days ago!'

Both guards turned their stares on Bianca.

'Bianca,' muttered Marco, tugging at her sleeve. 'I want to –'

'*I* want to return it,' said Bianca, keeping her voice steady and calm. 'I need to speak to the Duchess.'

'Thief!' snapped one of the guards, and he grabbed Bianca's wrist.

'Bianca!' Marco yelped, as the other guard seized his arm.

'You're both under arrest,' he said.

The guards dragged them in through the castle gate. 'It's fine,' Bianca murmured to Marco. 'It's part of the plan!'

'It'd better be,' Marco hissed back.

Bianca's heart skipped a beat at the sight of the courtyard, with its dark grey stones and dim doorways, its guards and servants milling around and its black banners fluttering from the walls. She realised with a shudder of dread that the guards must be taking them to the dungeons – and what if Filpepi and the Duke discovered her there before her mother did? They would waste no time in disposing of them. She had to get herself and Marco out of this.

She dug in her heels and shouted, at the top of her lungs, 'I must see the Duchess! She's in terrible danger!'

'Shut up!' yelled the guard.

'The Duchess needs to speak to me! She's in mortal danger.'

The servants in the courtyard turned and looked at her. Some put down their baskets and whispered to each other.

'We've come to warn the Duchess!' Marco's voice joined Bianca's. 'She's trusting the wrong people! We have to see her!'

Yes, that's it! Get their attention! Bianca grinned at Marco and went on shouting and pulling away from the guards. 'Please, the Duchess must see me!'

Soon everyone in the courtyard was staring at them. A crowd started to gather around the doorways and along the balcony that circled the courtyard. But some of them moved away once they caught sight of the youngsters, bored of the spectacle.

'Keep shouting,' Bianca said to Marco. 'We need to make a scene!'

'They can shout themselves hoarse in the cells,' one guard said, but he had to raise his voice to be heard over their cries, which only made the racket worse.

Bianca was starting to feel desperate. She had been so caught up in the idea of being reunited with her mother that she had rushed into things. 'Please, there's a traitor in the castle! Something terrible might happen if we don't talk to the Duchess!'

'Shut up, shut up!' The guard pushed her onwards towards the dungeons. Bianca tried to struggle; she needed to draw attention to herself as long as possible. But it was no use. The guard was strong, heaving her onwards. Tears rolled down her cheeks: she would never meet her mother; she would never fulfil the fate di Lombardi wanted for her.

As they entered the castle Bianca made one final desperate lurch, kicking the guard in the shins. Shaking him off, she ran back into the courtyard. But almost immediately the guard caught up with her, spinning her round, a look of fury etched across his face. He raised his hand to slap Bianca and she flinched away, squeezed her eyes shut and waited for the blow.

'Wait!'

The slap didn't come, and Bianca dared to open her eyes a tiny bit.

A pathway had cleared through the middle of the crowd. The servants and courtiers bowed as a dark-haired woman in a beautiful dark green dress passed them. It was the woman Bianca had seen in her sleepwalking visit. She wore a glittering silver tiara that shone on her forehead like a star that had fallen to earth. She was flanked by a group of tall men and women in long, sweeping dresses and robes.

'Duchess!' Bianca cried, and wriggled out of the surprised guard's hold to drop to her knees. Marco followed suit. 'Forgive me, but I have to speak to you!'

'Duchess Edita,' the guard said. 'Your Highness, please ignore these prisoners. They're simple thieves, just trying to get out of being taken to the dungeon.'

'I'll decide what they are, sergeant,' said Duchess Edita. Bianca looked up and met the woman's eyes. The Duchess walked slowly forward. 'What exactly do two thieves think I need to know so desperately?'

Bianca took a deep breath. 'My Lady, if you'll permit me, it's a bit of a long story.'

'Then shorten it,' said the Duchess.

Bianca's heart beat out a nervous rhythm as she spoke.

'Well . . . my friend and I come from a city called La Luminosa, a long way away.'

There was a flicker of something – Bianca didn't know what – on the Duchess's face when Bianca mentioned La Luminosa. Had the Duchess heard of it?

'I grew up in La Luminosa, but I recently discovered that I'm really from here . . . That is, my mother was. I was taken away from here as a baby. I was adopted by a man named Annunzio di Lombardi.'

There was a ripple of surprise and consternation among the Duchess's entourage. She held up her hand and they fell silent.

'Annunzio di Lombardi was a great man of Oscurita,' the Duchess Edita said slowly.

'In La Luminosa he was known as a great artist,' Bianca said. 'He brought me up as his apprentice, but he told me I'd been a foundling. I only discovered the truth when he died.'

Another gasp, louder this time, echoed around the courtyard.

'He is dead?' asked the Duchess, her voice perfectly level.

'Poisoned,' said Marco. 'By traitors who tried to steal *our* Duchess's crown.'

'He left me a black medallion, and a letter that explained that my mother was from Oscurita,' said Bianca.

'A medallion?' said the Duchess. Her eyes were wide and dark.

'Yes, Your Highness. And, you see . . .' Bianca swallowed. *It's all or nothing, now.* 'I think my mother . . . might be you.' Bianca climbed slowly to her feet. She tried to steady her trembling hands as she met the gaze of the Duchess of Oscurita. 'Please, did you give a child to Annunzio di Lombardi to hide away, twelve years ago?'

'How dare you?' the guard yelled. He raised his spear. 'Your Highness, let me teach this insolent thief a lesson!'

'What is she accused of stealing?' the Duchess asked. There was a tremor in her voice. Bianca's heart beat wildly.

'This, Your Highness,' said the other guard. He moved forward and handed the small silver bracelet to the Duchess with a low bow.

Duchess Edita took it from him, turning it over and over between her fingers. She looked at the bracelet, then looked at Bianca. Then her delicate hands flew to her mouth and her expression melted. Her hands dropped to reveal a soft smile.

'You may release them, sergeant. This girl is no thief.'

Bianca could hardly breathe. She met the Duchess's eyes and felt her own start to well with tears.

'But Your Highness, the bracelet –'

'Belongs to her,' said Edita. Behind her, the courtiers broke out into unrestrained chatter. 'This bracelet is all I had left of my daughter. But now I have her back . . . The lost Lady Bianca.'

Bianca's eyes filled with tears and the Duchess's face swam in front of her. 'Mother?' she whispered.

Edita took Bianca's hands in hers. 'My darling Bianca, can it really be you? Let me look at you.' She stroked a strand of hair back from Bianca's face. 'I can't believe it. After all this time. And Annunzio is dead . . .'

Bianca couldn't speak, so she nodded.

'She has returned at last,' Edita cried, spinning Bianca around to face the courtiers. 'My daughter, Bianca!' called Edita. 'The future Duchess of Oscurita!'

Bianca's knees turned to jelly, and she stumbled backwards, but a pair of strong arms caught and held her.

Duchess Edita dropped to her knees in a pool of spreading green silk and pulled Bianca into a tearful embrace. Bianca threw her arms around her mother's neck and held her so tightly she thought she would never, ever let go.

Chapter Thirteen

Bianca shifted on the garden bench, digging her fingers under the tightly laced corset of her gown, trying to find the place beneath her left arm where it kept poking her. If she could just work out which bit of it was the culprit, she might be able to tuck some of the fabric between it and her as a cushion. It wasn't as if this dress didn't have plenty of fabric to go around – she felt slightly lost in its deep blue oceans of silk and mountains of silver lace.

'Lady Bianca, please,' said Lady Margherita. 'You must not fidget so.'

'Sorry,' said Bianca.

Beside her, Marco heaved a deep sigh and Lady Margherita shot him a glance of pure disdain.

Marco was looking almost as fancy as Bianca was, in a high-necked doublet of black on black on black. But she knew that even if her dress was horribly uncomfortable, she looked pretty amazing, whereas Marco just looked ill. The stiff black cloth didn't suit him at all, and the artificial lighting of Oscurita wasn't doing him any favours – his healthy brown skin glowed in the sunlight of La Luminosa,

130

but after two days in Oscurita it looked sallow and dull.

Bianca tried to sit back and enjoy the little garden that came with her new suite of rooms in the Castle of Oscurita. It really was a wonderful place, crowded with statues of sprites and trickling fountains and strange plants she'd never seen before. An arbour covered in black ivy with bright pink flowers curved over the bench where she and Marco were sitting, and all around the walls *lux aurumque* flowers grew in beds full of shifting, flickering light.

It was one of the most beautiful places Bianca had ever been. It was just a shame that she was so *bored*.

She reached out a hand and turned the head of a *lux aurumque* flower towards her, watching the way the shadows swayed as she moved it.

Making magical paints had been one of the most thrilling accomplishments in her life. A secret only she knew. A thought – instant and unwelcome – came into her head about the apprentices she'd left behind. Had her apprentices run out of magical paint yet? Would the studio still be running? Would the apprentices be worried about her?

Doubt it, Bianca thought bitterly. *They don't need me.*

'Bianca, put that down! You'll dirty your hands.'

Bianca looked at the stain the *lux aurumque* petals had left on her fingertips.

Lady Margherita snapped, 'You are a lady, not a gardener!'

Bianca frowned at Lady Margherita. She was an older lady who'd been assigned as Bianca's chaperone. Bianca wasn't sure what a chaperone was supposed to do, but so far they'd been in Oscurita for two days and all Lady Margherita had done was correct her behaviour, her posture and her speech, glare at Marco as if he was some kind of peasant rogue who might kidnap Bianca at any minute, and above all make sure that Bianca never actually did anything interesting. She dressed all in black, without a hint of colour anywhere on her, including in her ghostly-pale skin.

'Lady Margherita,' Bianca said, 'can't I –'

'Ah?' Lady Margherita held up a warning finger. Bianca briefly fantasised about chopping it off.

'*May* I see my mother today?' she asked carefully.

'Sit up straight and ask again,' said Lady Margherita.

Bianca suppressed the urge to argue. She was already learning to pick her battles. She straightened up, making the corset dig deeper into her side, and said, 'May I see my mother please?' in a clear, polite tone.

'Her Royal Highness Duchess Edita is very busy,' said Lady Margherita, without looking up from her embroidery.

Bianca and Marco rolled their eyes at each other. Duchess Edita was always busy – or very busy, or extremely busy, or not available right now, or completely otherwise indisposed. Bianca understood that her mother was a Duchess and had duties to her city and her people . . . but still, surely she could take a few minutes to spend time with her long-lost daughter?

Bianca was sure it wasn't Duchess Edita's fault – she imagined an army of Lady Margheritas and Secretary Francos ganging up on her, keeping Bianca away. None of the court seemed to like Bianca very much, and she knew they all thought Marco was suspiciously foreign and not a suitable companion for a member of the royal family.

'Why don't we go for a walk?' Marco suggested. 'We could see more of the city. Aren't royals supposed to know about the places they rule over?'

Bianca gave him a grateful smile. 'That's a wonderful idea,' she said.

'Absolutely not,' said Lady Margherita.

'Of course not,' Marco whispered.

'It's not safe,' Lady Margherita went on. 'Not for a lady such as yourself – there could be assassins and vagabonds flooding the city as we speak, just waiting to take advantage of your naivety! And moreover, you might get into trouble. Nobody here has forgotten that you were dragged into the castle as common thieves!' She fixed her glare on Marco again. 'As your chaperone, I won't let you get talked into anything so . . . *low*.'

'Well, we won't go walking then!' Bianca said, as brightly as she could manage. 'Can I – *may I* at least do some painting? I'd love to try to capture this garden. And I was thinking I could paint a portrait of my mother, and –'

'Paint?' Lady Margherita looked scandalised. 'Why would you want to paint? You would stain your dress and your fingernails and . . . no. Painting is not a pastime for a lady.'

'In La Luminosa, I gave Duchess Catriona herself painting lessons!' Bianca said, raising her chin and trying not to remember how few of the Duchess's art lessons had actually got as far as painting. But Bianca did miss her friend.

'Well, in Oscurita, your mother the Duchess would never turn her hand to anything so messy.' Lady Margherita put down her embroidery with a sigh of suppressed annoyance that almost matched the one building inside Bianca. 'Lady Bianca, is there something wrong? It's as if you don't like it here!'

Bianca shook her head. 'I love Oscurita! It's just . . . surely even ladies have to have something to *do*.'

'If you really can't just sit still and enjoy the garden, why don't we go through our deportment basics again, hmm?'

It seemed to be the best offer Bianca was going to get. She got up and stretched.

'No!' Lady Margherita snapped. 'Sit!'

Bianca sat. She avoided Marco's eyes; she knew exactly what he'd say about her following orders like a dog.

'You *must* learn to rise like a lady! Don't spring to your feet as if you've found a needle on your chair. Remember, you are a future Duchess – time itself will wait for you if you command it.'

Bianca took a deep breath and then got up as slowly and gracefully as she could.

'Now, let's see you walk,' said Lady Margherita. She folded her hands in her lap, giving Bianca her undivided attention. Bianca glanced at Marco. He grinned and made an elaborate, sweeping '*go on*' gesture.

Bianca took a few steps, her back straight, her head up, her hands held neatly but not too tightly in front of her. She walked as far as the trickling fountain and gazed down into the dark water. Then she turned and walked back to the bench.

'No, no, no,' muttered Lady Margherita. 'You still walk like a peasant, child. Fold your hands more neatly. Keep your chin up – not that far! Keep your skirt out of the flowers, but don't fiddle with it. You must make it look *natural*.'

Bianca turned a little so she was facing Marco, with her back to Lady Margherita. 'Can you imagine Duchess Catriona putting up with this?' she whispered.

Marco sniggered. 'Not on your life!'

'Marco Xavier! What are you saying to Lady Bianca?' Bianca stood back as Lady Margherita leapt to her feet, completely ignoring her own rules about sitting. 'I have half a mind to have you thrown out of the castle!'

No! Bianca felt her face flush. *I definitely can't cope with all this on my own!*

'Lady Margherita,' she said, drawing herself up as tall as she could. She thought, *what would Duchess Catriona do?* 'Fetch me my embroidery,' she commanded. When Lady Margherita opened her mouth, Bianca cut her off with her best impression of Catriona's withering glare. 'It is my desire. And in case you've forgotten, my desire is your command.'

Lady Margherita raised an eyebrow, but she curtseyed low and scurried away.

As soon as she was gone, Bianca let out a heavy sigh and sank to her knees. The stiff silk of her skirt ballooned around her and she tried to pat it down but it only seemed to inflate somewhere else.

Marco got to his feet. 'Come on, let's get out of here and back to La Luminosa before she comes back!'

Bianca frowned up at him. 'I can't go back! I haven't even had a chance to explain about the Baron to anyone who'll listen yet. What about my mother?'

135

'What about my father? Two whole days, Bianca!' Marco sank back down on the bench and stared at his hands in the flickering light from the flowers and the dim thunder-lamp on the wall. 'We've been staying in this place for two days and I didn't even get the chance to tell Father I was going to meet you, let alone run off to a completely different, horrible world!'

Bianca gasped. 'It is not horrible!'

Marco raised his eyebrows. 'You hate it here just as much as I do!'

'I do not!' Bianca protested. *I don't*, she added to herself. *Not as much as he does.*

'Oh *right*.' Marco scoffed. 'You like the way Lady Deportment treats you, do you? And the rest of the court? They all look at us like we're . . .' He flailed his hands, looking for the right word.

They look at us like we don't belong here, she thought. On their first evening in Oscurita they'd attended a grand dinner in their honour that had felt more like a funeral feast. It wasn't just the black clothes and the dim light – Bianca still thought the castle was beautiful. It was the way the courtiers sat and whispered together. Some remembered to smile when they spoke directly to Bianca, but they gave each other odd looks and shushed each other when she met them in the corridors.

Bianca sighed. 'I know, it's all a bit strange. But I can't just leave!'

'So you enjoy your lessons in royalty? You like learning to sit and walk and not being allowed to touch your own garden? You like the idea of never painting again?'

136

Bianca flinched as if he'd jabbed her in the stomach. 'No, of course not! None of this is me, you know that. But I'm sure if I can just talk to my mother –'

'Bianca, your mother hasn't bothered to spend more than two minutes with you since you arrived.'

Tears sprang to Bianca's eyes. She struggled to her feet and stepped back, hoping the dim light would hide her face from Marco's limited vision.

'Come with me,' Marco insisted. 'Come *home*. You're not happy here.'

'I am *extremely* happy here!' Bianca snapped. The lie caught in her throat, and her thoughts echoed back: *I want to be happy here* . . . She sniffed back the tears and turned on Marco, her face flushing. Much as she missed La Luminosa, there was no way she was leaving. 'This is where I belong, and this is where I'm staying.'

'Well, I'm going. At least I know my father will be glad to see me.'

It was as if she'd been skewered right through the heart with a shard of ice. 'I bet your father hasn't even noticed you've gone,' she snarled. She felt the next sentence before she said it, rising behind her teeth like water behind a dam. 'Who'd miss a tumbler who can't stand heights?'

Marco glared at her from underneath his eyebrows. 'Lady Margherita's wrong,' he said slowly. 'You *have* changed since you came here. You've forgotten everything you care about. What about Duchess Catriona? What about the other apprentices? What are they going to do if the only one who knows how to make magical paints has swanned off to play at being a royal? What about di Lombardi's legacy?'

With every word Bianca's heart beat faster and faster. Catriona, Cosimo, Rosa, Lucia, di Lombardi, Marco, her mother – how was she supposed to serve them all at once?

'I've got to try!' she said. 'I've only just found my mother! I just . . . I don't care about di Lombardi's legacy right now!'

The words felt like poison in her mouth but she raised her chin at Marco defiantly.

'I see. I'd better go, then,' Marco said. 'You'll have to open a painting for me.'

Bianca sucked in a deep breath. She wished she could take back everything she'd just said. But she nodded. 'Margherita will be looking for my embroidery for a while. It's not in my room – I dropped it behind the bench over there.'

For a second they grinned at each other – watery, strained grins.

'Come on. There are some paintings in my drawing room; I'll see if I can get one to open.'

She led the way back inside, through the tall door set with thick, distorting glass and into her private drawing room. She sighed as she looked at the huge room. Three enormous couches surrounded a fireplace nearly as big as her attic back in di Lombardi's old house. In the hearth, twisted black wood gave off bright blue flames that heated and lit the room – but not enough to keep Marco from shivering or tripping over the black marble tables and piles of silky purple cushions.

Bianca had felt a little bit lost and alone in this room even with Marco around. She could barely imagine it without him.

Then she scolded herself. *If he wants to go, let him go. I'll be perfectly fine. I'm home now.*

Most of the paintings in the room were portraits of people who looked faintly familiar – they had to be old relatives, but she hadn't been able to talk to her mother long enough to find out about them. Only one had a door: a portrait of an old lady with hair as white as snow, wearing a deep crimson robe embroidered with a white dragon. She was standing, leaning on a cane and looking out of a high window. The door was black, just like the one that'd led Bianca to Oscurita, except instead of blue trim, it had bright red edges, the colour of a La Luminosa rose.

Bianca ran her fingers over the door within the painting. The painting didn't have much depth, but she could definitely feel something solid. She pulled the paintbrush from the jewelled purse that hung over her shoulder and held it up to her lips. 'Hidden rooms, secret passages, second city,' she whispered, and the familiar *clickclickclick* sound began as the tiny copper key unfolded from its hiding place inside the handle of the brush.

Bianca's heart sank, despite herself, when the key fitted easily into the lock. The door swung open to reveal the familiar maze of passages. Their dim, flickering torchlight seemed bright in comparison to the permanent darkness of Oscurita.

'Wow,' said Marco softly. Bianca turned to see him holding the map to the passages. While she'd been opening the door he had slipped away to fetch his bag. She felt a stab of heartache when she realised it must have already been packed.

Marco held out the map so she could see that another

line had magically appeared – this one shooting off from another passage into what looked like the fields to the north of the city.

'So opening doors here puts their doors into the passages,' Marco muttered. 'That's amazing. Master di Lombardi was a genius.'

Bianca nodded silently.

Marco rolled up the map and shouldered his bag. 'I'll be off then.'

'All right,' Bianca said. She didn't mean it to come out as a whisper, but it did.

Marco put one foot through the door, and then suddenly turned back to face Bianca. 'You have to come back to La Luminosa,' he said. 'At least visit. Soon. Promise?'

'I promise,' Bianca said.

'Because only you can open the doors. I can't come back here without that key,' Marco went on. 'If you don't come back we'll never see each other again.'

'OK!' Bianca felt a smile stretch across her face, and it was as if someone had lit a bright torch in a dark room. 'I really promise.' She hesitated, and then grabbed Marco into a hug.

'I'll always be around if you need me,' Marco muttered. Then he pulled away and climbed into the painting. Bianca waved, and he waved back, and then the door closed between them.

Bianca went back to her private garden and sat staring into the trickling fountain for a few minutes, waiting for

Lady Margherita to realise her embroidery wasn't in her room. But instead of being cross and red-faced, when her chaperone burst back into the garden she looked even paler than before – her cheeks were white as bleached bone.

She laid eyes on Bianca and clutched at her heart as if she was having an attack.

'Lady Bianca, I am very, very sorry to have left you alone for so long!'

Bianca blinked, surprised by Lady Margherita's sincerely worried expression. In fact, her chaperone actually looked a little . . . scared.

Could she really be that worried about not finding a bit of sewing? Bianca's heart thawed – maybe her attempt to impersonate Duchess Catriona's intimidating glare had been much more successful than she'd thought.

'Oh Lady Margherita, I'm glad you're back,' she said. 'I found my embroidery. It was here all the time. I'm so sorry I sent you on a wild goose chase.'

Lady Margherita nodded, her heaving chest starting to slow. 'I'm just glad nothing untoward happened to you while you were alone with that . . . that boy. Where is he, anyway?'

'He left,' Bianca said quietly. 'He . . . we decided it was time for him to go home.'

'Oh! Well, I really think that's for the best, don't you?' Lady Margherita said, brightening considerably. 'Now, let's see your needlework.'

She settled down on the bench and Bianca reluctantly joined her and fished out the rumpled, knot-ridden embroidery.

It was a black handkerchief that she was supposed to be edging with a bright golden flame pattern – but her flames looked more like jagged shards of glass.

She saw Lady Margherita cringe, but then rein in her reaction.

'That's very . . . interesting, Your Highness. But I'm sure you can do better. Why don't you unpick it and start again?'

After a few minutes of work, Lady Margherita spoke again.

'Yes, that's right, if you find a knot just snip it with the scissors. Oh, and Lady Bianca . . . there's no need to tell your mother that I left you alone for so long,' she added, in an overly bright and cheery tone of voice. 'You know she worries so. But nothing happened, so there's no need to say more about it, is there?'

'No, no need at all,' Bianca said. She felt Lady Margherita relax beside her.

Bianca shook her head and bent over her needlework. She had to admit, Marco was right about the odd way things were done here. *What did she think I could get up to by myself for a few minutes?* she wondered. *Or did she really think Marco was secretly an assassin?*

Bianca tried to focus on her sewing, but everything she did seemed to make it worse. It was so frustrating she started to fantasise about running over to one of the torches and setting fire to the stupid thing. If it'd just been boring, repetitive work it might not have been so bad – Bianca had spent plenty of hours trying to mix exactly the right blue or painting a hundred perfectly even lines of brickwork onto a picture.

But, unlike the embroidery, those things she'd been able to do; she'd accomplished something.

What if they really won't let me paint ever again?

She couldn't think like that. She just had to wait, then her mother would talk to her and everything would be fine.

Bianca used her embroidery scissors to snip a few of the *lux aurumque* flowers while Lady Margherita wasn't looking. She slipped them quickly into her jewelled purse. She was just wondering if she might have time to experiment with making her own magical paints later when she heard the clicking of several pairs of delicate shoes on stone. She turned, and her heart skipped a beat at the sight of Duchess Edita, flanked by a group of courtiers. The long, sweeping gowns that hid their feet made them look a bit like ghosts floating into the garden.

'Curtsey!' hissed Lady Margherita, snatching the embroidery from Bianca's hand.

Bianca got to her feet and dropped into the most graceful curtsey she could manage. It wasn't very graceful.

'Your Royal Highness,' Bianca said meekly. She kept her head down, waiting for Duchess Edita to speak.

This isn't what I thought having a mother would be like. She hadn't dared to expect much – she'd thought her mother might reject her or even have her thrown in jail. But to accept her as the lost princess and then leave her here, bound up in beautiful gowns and guarded by a chaperone . . .

Duchess Edita didn't speak, and the blood flushed to Bianca's cheeks as she stared down at the grey stone. How long should she stay like this? She hadn't been told the protocol for looking up if the Duchess didn't give her permission.

Then a purple gown swept into view under her nose. Duchess Edita reached out and touched Bianca's face, slowly raising her chin until she was standing up straight and looking into her mother's eyes.

The Duchess smiled softly. 'My dear, I'm so sorry. Come, sit.' She took Bianca's elbow and led her to another bench. They sat together, and Edita slipped her arm around Bianca. Bianca felt all the tension of the last few days falling away, and she started to well up again as she smiled at her mother.

'I've wanted to talk to you,' she said.

'Oh, me too,' said Duchess Edita. 'I'm sorry I haven't been able to spend much time with you. I've been so busy. I'm sorry to say that Oscurita is not the safe, happy place it once was. But let's not talk about that now . . . I want to talk about *you*! How are you, my love?'

'Oh, I'm . . . I'm very well,' said Bianca.

Duchess Edita frowned. 'Truly?'

'Everything's marvellous,' Bianca said, but she heard the tightening in her own throat as she said it, and Duchess Edita obviously heard it too. Her eyebrows twitched. She stared at Bianca for a second, and Bianca felt as if everything she was feeling was written across her face in bright red paint.

Duchess Edita looked up and smiled at her entourage. 'I think we need to have a chat. Mother to daughter.'

Bianca felt her heart lift as the Duchess's courtiers and Lady Margherita curtseyed and bowed out of the garden.

Duchess Edita put her arms around Bianca and hugged

her close, wrapping her up in folds of purple silk and strands of dark, flowing hair.

'Tell me everything, darling,' she said. 'I've been terrible to leave you alone this long. I want to know everything about you.'

Bianca smiled as she looked into her mother's deep brown eyes. *This is all I ever wanted.* Bianca would give up everything to stay here, like this, with her mother.

Chapter Fourteen

'But the smoke was too much for him,' Bianca said, sniffing back tears. 'And he died. He was poisoned by the traitors. The ones I've been trying to –'

'How *terrible*,' Duchess Edita said. 'My poor dear di Lombardi. And he never told you anything about where you'd come from or about your family?'

'Nothing,' said Bianca. 'Until he left me a message in his will.'

'And the medallion?' Duchess Edita asked. 'That was when he left you the medallion, too?'

'Yes,' Bianca said. 'The message showed you giving me to him, and then it showed me growing up in La Luminosa and coming back here with the medallion. Then it turned into a map so I could find my way between the magic paintings to the one that opens into Oscurita.'

'And you came,' said Duchess Edita. She looked away, but Bianca saw the tear as it rolled down her cheek before she wiped it away. She turned back and clasped Bianca's hands in hers. 'I can't believe it – my daughter, so clever, so talented. I'll never forget di Lombardi's kindness in helping return you to me. And saving my medallion, too.'

'The medallion's yours?' Bianca asked.

'Oh yes. You see, it's not just a piece of jewellery. It will help me secure the safety of Oscurita! Did you bring it with you?'

Bianca flushed. 'I thought it was safer to leave it in La Luminosa. The Baron –'

'Well, never mind!' Duchess Edita pulled Bianca close again and planted a kiss on her cheek. 'Perhaps one day you can fetch it. But not now. The medallion means nothing, as long as we're together.'

Bianca smiled into her mother's shoulder. Despite the corset and the embroidery and the curtseying, she would never regret coming to Oscurita.

A low, resounding bell rang out and Duchess Edita pulled away. 'I must go, it's time to dress for dinner. I'll see you there, darling.' She kissed Bianca's cheek again and left her alone in the garden, watching the flickering lights of the *lux aurumque* flowers and breathing more deeply and calmly than she had for days.

'Now, remember your protocol,' said Lady Margherita, walking a few steps ahead of Bianca as they approached the great hall. 'Stand whenever the Duchess stands. Speak equally to the people sitting on either side of you. Be careful not to confuse your cutlery, and never drink with your left hand.'

Bianca nodded, but she wasn't really listening – almost all her concentration was focused on just walking in a straight line in the incredible gown she'd been strapped into. She thought she'd been stiffly bound up with lace and corsets and stockings before, but now she realised that had just been practice. This evening, Lady Margherita had presented her with a dress that was as beautiful as anything she'd ever seen Duchess Catriona wear, but weighed almost as much as she did. The corset kept her back pulled up straight and the layers of underskirts felt like walking through a field of silk with every step. The long lines of the flowing bright blue gown made her feel tall and lithe – neither of which she'd ever felt before – and the heavy dark blue velvet coat dragged her shoulders back and down. And then on top of that, her forehead and neck and arms wore a jingling waterfall of silver chains dripping with sapphires and onyx and glittering diamonds.

'You look like a real princess,' said Lady Margherita with a genuine smile as they reached the door to the great hall.

'I feel like one, too,' said Bianca. *Apparently real princesses feel like they're about to topple over*, she added, but only inside her head.

The doors swung open.

'Her Royal Highness, Lady Bianca di Oscurita,' announced the footman. A few of the courtiers whispered to each other or turned their heads away, while others smirked a bit too widely.

She stepped inside, keeping her back tall and trying to walk with confidence, and looked up at the high table at the far end of the room to find her mother.

She was sitting between two men, their heads bent close

together so Bianca couldn't make out any of their faces. The Duchess was listening to some intense counsel. Then one of the men pushed back his black hair from his forehead. Bianca's stomach dropped into the pointy toes of her velvet shoes.

It was the traitor, Filpepi.

Bianca picked up her heavy skirts and ran the last few feet to the high table.

'. . . patience,' she heard her mother say. 'There's no profit in rushing this.'

'But Your Highness, we must begin soon,' said the other man.

The Baron da Russo.

'You!' Bianca yelled. A mutter of shock and scandal went up from the courtiers, but Bianca ignored them.

'Bianca! Are you all right?' Duchess Edita asked as Bianca approached the high table.

Bianca sucked in the deepest breath she could manage – the corset was laced so tight she was barely able to breathe even if she *wasn't* trying to run. 'Mother, these two are traitors! The two traitors I tried to tell you about! They're criminals! They –' She paused to gasp, silently cursing whatever idiot had come up with the idea of corsets in the first place. 'They only want power!' She glared at Filpepi. 'Don't you remember me, Filpepi? '

Filpepi said nothing, but gazed calmly at Bianca, a supercilious smile playing on his lips. The Baron puffed out a heavy sigh.

'Duchess Edita, this girl knows nothing,' he said.

'Don't listen to them!' Bianca pleaded. 'They killed Master di Lombardi, and they tried to kill the Duchess of La Luminosa!'

A gasp of shock echoed around the room.

'Silence!' Duchess Edita commanded, getting to her feet. The court instantly fell silent, until the only sound was the rasping of Bianca's breath in her throat. 'I won't have my court disrupted by such talk. Filpepi, da Russo – I think it's best if you leave for now.'

The two traitors rose and bowed deeply to Duchess Edita. Bianca felt sick as they smiled to each other and walked out of the hall.

'Send the guards after them!' she said. 'Who knows what damage they can do in the castle if they're not watched?'

'Bianca, I won't imprison or spy on any of my subjects without knowing what crime they're supposed to have committed. Why don't you sit down and tell me everything?'

Bianca sank into the chair beside her mother. 'I've told you most of it already – you just didn't know they were the ones I was talking about! They were going to kill Duchess Catriona, and they poisoned di Lombardi *and* tried to burn him alive. Marco and I would have died in that fire too if di Lombardi hadn't shown us the way out!' Before she could go on, her mother reached over and took her hands.

'These crimes sound terrible!' Bianca's shoulders sagged with relief. But her mother hadn't finished. 'But they were not committed here. I understand you are fond of the City of Light, but it isn't even in my world, let alone within my power.'

Bianca's jaw dropped. 'How can you just let them get away with murder? Simply because it happened in La Luminosa and not Oscurita?'

'That is the way it is, sweetest,' Edita said, reaching up to stroke back one of the elaborate braids in Bianca's hair that had untwisted itself.

'But, Mother,' Bianca pleaded. 'If they betrayed Duchess Catriona for her throne, how do you know they aren't plotting to steal yours too?'

'Ah, if they showed any sign they were traitors to *Oscurita*, then I certainly could do whatever I liked with them,' said Duchess Edita. 'But I don't believe they will.'

'Why on earth not?' Bianca asked, feeling totally at a loss.

'The Baron and Filpepi were visitors to La Luminosa, but they are citizens of Oscurita – just like you are now. They felt no loyalty to the little child duchess in the City of Light – but they have always been exceptionally loyal to me.'

'I can't believe it,' Bianca muttered.

'I don't have to just believe,' said Edita gently. 'They've both proved themselves to me. How much did Annunzio tell you about the Civil War?'

'Nothing,' Bianca said. Then she remembered the first few scenes of the painting. 'But the story did show the city under attack when you smuggled me out. What happened?'

'Only a few days after you were born, a vile pretender to the throne took the opportunity to attack me. I sent you with Annunzio because I was afraid you were their next target. Years of war tore the city apart. Even now, supporters of the pretender lurk in the city, plotting to kill me and take my throne. During the war, the Baron da Russo and Master Filpepi both proved their loyalty to me many times over.'

'But how?' Bianca asked.

Duchess Edita shook her head. 'You don't want to hear those stories,' she said. 'They're not for children.'

'I do!' Bianca protested. 'How can I trust that they're really loyal if I don't know the truth?'

Her mother looked at her and smiled softly. 'Dearest, you trust *me*, don't you?'

'Well, yes . . . but –'

Duchess Edita snapped her fingers, and Lady Margherita materialised by her elbow. 'Lady Margherita, I think Lady Bianca would rather have her dinner in her rooms tonight,' she said.

Bianca bristled – wasn't her mother even going to ask how she felt about it?

The weight of her outfit seemed to double as she let Lady Margherita escort her out of the great hall. It took almost as long to get her out of it as she'd actually spent wearing it, but as soon as she could do without Lady Margherita's help Bianca shooed her out of the room with her best imperious glare.

She paced the room, strewing underskirts and slinging silver chains over the backs of chairs and the edges of mirrors, until she was down to the base layer and she could finally move freely. She sank down on the edge of her bed, clenched her fists in the black and purple silk eiderdown and punched the feather pillows.

This wasn't right, not at all. She had to believe her mother's statement that Baron da Russo and Filpepi had been loyal citizens of Oscurita, once. But they'd been loyal to La Luminosa too, or pretended to be. The Baron had even been Duchess Catriona's regent, in charge of running the city until she came of age. He'd bided his time. The Baron was a *schemer*. Whatever he was doing, he'd be in it for the long haul. Bianca knew it in her bones. One day, maybe not this week or this year, but one day, he would work his schemes on her mother too.

She got up and walked through to her drawing room, looking out through the distorting glass to the faint glow of the *lux aurumque* flowers in the garden beyond.

If only she could prove just how long the Baron had been scheming with Filpepi to take over La Luminosa, if she could just show her mother *why* they were on the run . . .

Bianca turned, slowly, looking up at the painting of the old lady with the white hair.

They're on the run. That's it.

Filpepi and the Baron had escaped to Oscurita with Captain Raphaeli and the palace guards right on their heels – and she knew for a fact that Filpepi's study had been left just as it was, because clearing it was a job she'd been avoiding!

If she searched his room, and the Baron's room at the palace, maybe she could find some evidence that would sway her mother. Maybe whatever they were planning could be stopped before they could put it in motion!

It had to be worth a try.

Bianca hurried back to her room and changed into her

old dress. She tipped out the contents of the jewelled purse and stuck the paintbrush key into her pocket. She paused, picking up the *lux aurumque* flower she'd snipped from its stem in the garden earlier. It obviously held a life force of its own, because the petals were still fleshy and glowing, casting a shifting golden light around the room. She smelled it – its scent was strange, a bit like a sunflower, with a strange undertone of *ether* and heavy oils. She carefully slipped it into her pocket as she opened the door behind the dragon lady.

'I'll be back,' she promised herself, as if she was speaking to the old lady. 'I'll come back and make those traitors pay for what they did to Master di Lombardi.'

The old lady didn't move, but Bianca could almost imagine that her half-smile was a sign of approval.

She stepped into the passages and closed the door behind her.

Chapter Fifteen

As soon as she was in the passages, Bianca realised her mistake.

'Marco's got the map,' she groaned. Slumping against the wall, she ran her fingers over its stone-cool and canvas-scented surface. She hadn't noticed before, but the range of colours spattered over the walls were a bit different here – there were more greys and dark colours, and at the same time the bright colours and the glimmering sparks of light were even brighter. Perhaps she'd come out in the palace if she went through a door surrounded by sun-bleached stone, copper, pale shady blues and greens and terracotta.

'At least there's only one way to go,' she sighed, and set off away from the black and red door.

She wandered down quite a long stretch of passage before there were any more doors, and when her corridor finally opened onto a crossroads, she didn't recognise any of the paintings she looked out through. She seemed to be in a complex, twisting path of people's private houses, and it wouldn't help her to get caught climbing out of a portrait of someone's grandmother.

What's more, it was night-time – the night-lamps and the starlight still made La Luminosa brighter than Oscurita, but it meant she couldn't just go leaping out of paintings into people's bedrooms and hoping for the best.

Finally, when it seemed as if she'd been walking for hours, she turned into a corridor and felt a spark of familiarity. She'd been here. But where was she? From beyond a heavy iron door, she heard a ticking noise, like a clock. A low bell rang out, just once.

Of course – the Via del Orologica, the street of clockmakers! That was all the way across La Luminosa, but if this was where she and Marco had been exploring before they'd found their way to Oscurita, that meant that the door on the other side . . .

She leapt across the corridor and pressed her face to the glass panel in the door. *Yes!* There were the dancers, trailing coloured silk as they spun and swirled around the great golden throne. And beyond them, she could see into the Museum of Art.

But Bianca frowned. The Museum was empty and dark. The night-lamps hadn't been lit, and even the guards who normally stood by the paintings all night had gone.

She peered through the doorway again, and this time she noticed a sign, illuminated by the starlight:

TOMORROW HER ROYAL MAJESTY
DUCHESS CATRIONA DI LA LUMINOSA
WILL JUDGE THE FINAL ENTRIES IN HER
MAJESTY'S COMPETITION

TO CHOOSE THE NEW ROYAL-ARTIST-IN-RESIDENCE AND MASTER OF THE STUDIOS

A surge of dread paralysed her to the spot. She'd forgotten about the competition. It was far too late for her to enter now. She expected to feel relieved – after all, the studio had been too much for her, hadn't it? But instead, she just felt guilty and sad – especially when she thought of how much faith Catriona had placed in her. She was supposed to be di Lombardi's successor, and she hadn't painted *anything* in days. But it was more than that. Art was what defined her, her whole world, until she'd found out that her mother was alive. And she had just given that up. Was it something she could only do if she chose La Luminosa over her own mother?

And you're the only one who knows the magic paint recipes, said a voice at the back of her mind. *You left your studio without even giving them instructions. You ran away to play at being a princess in a magic castle.*

Bianca shuddered violently. It was true, she shouldn't have left them like she did. But who wouldn't have run away if it meant meeting their mother for the very first time?

A heavy feeling settled in the pit of Bianca's stomach and she slid to the floor, her back against the painted stone passage wall.

Could she really go back to the studio, rummage through Filpepi's things and then vanish again, without stopping to help the other apprentices? But it would take months to teach them everything she knew, and she couldn't leave

Filpepi and the Baron free in Oscurita when she guessed they were up to no good.

She pulled the paintbrush and the flower from her pockets and stared at them until her eyes stung.

Master di Lombardi, help me. Should I go back? I didn't tell Edita where I was going; won't she worry? But I didn't tell Catriona where I was going, either. Or Cosimo, or Rosa, or Master Xavier.

Even Marco's angry with me.

'I've made a huge mess of all of this,' she muttered. She knew she didn't belong in La Luminosa, but everything she loved was here. And she wanted to belong in Oscurita, except nobody but her mother seemed to even want *her*.

Bong, bong, bong, bong, bong, bong, bong, bong, bong, bong.

Bianca shivered as the bell from the Via del Orologico rang out the time.

Ten o'clock.

There was just one place she could go to get her head straight, somewhere that didn't feel like it belonged to either Catriona or Edita.

Master di Lombardi's private studio.

She hurried along the corridors, partly remembering and partly feeling her way, until she turned down a dim corridor to find the door into the studio. Stepping into the bright room, she felt a little calmer as she looked at the paintings and contraptions she'd been working on. She might not feel completely at home in either city, but this place in the no-man's-land of the passages was hers, as surely as it'd been di Lombardi's.

Bianca's eyes fell on a charcoal self-portrait she'd begun a few days ago, and she hesitated, surprised by how much it looked like her mother, and not herself at all.

The picture seemed to call to her. It wasn't magic – it was something even more powerfully tempting. It was the urge to draw something. *Anything*.

Maybe if I finish this quickly I'll feel better, she thought. She'd certainly be able to strike 'perhaps I'm not even an artist any more' off her growing list of anxieties.

I'll do this, and then I'll go back to Oscurita and let them know I am safe. She seized a stick of charcoal and started to sketch in more lines, adding just a few small wrinkles and changing the shape of the hair to make it look all the more like her mother. *I'll put everything right in both cities*, she thought as she worked. She'd apologise to her mother for running off like a child. Then she'd apologise to the Duchess Catriona for abandoning her too. She'd search Filpepi's studio for proof of his evil deeds, then go back to Oscurita and show it to her mother. She could write the definitive work on magical paints while she was living in her mother's palace and give it to Cosimo when it was done.

She found herself smiling as she filled in a shadow beneath her mother's lips. *That actually sounds like a plan.*

Just as she was raising her charcoal towards her mother's eye . . . it blinked.

Bianca dropped the charcoal.

'B-Bianca?' the picture said, in a voice that was like her mother's but had a strange rasping tone like the sound of charcoal being dragged over paper. Bianca took a step back and stared as the picture came to life, bit by bit – first the eyes, then the lips, then the rest, until it was as if her mother was looking out at her. She gasped and her lips trembled. 'Bianca! Thank goodness, you're there!'

'I'm here. I'm sorry I didn't tell you where I was going,' Bianca said. She stared into her mother's dark eyes as they blinked at her. 'I . . . I didn't even use any magic!' she gasped. 'How are you doing this?'

The drawing of Edita smiled sadly. 'The bond between us is strong, my love. But there's no time, I can't keep this up for long. I need your help!'

'What? What's wrong?'

'I'm so sorry, darling – you were right about the Baron, and that traitor Filpepi!'

'I knew it!' Bianca clenched her fists, wishing she could reach into the drawing to embrace her mother. 'Are you all right?'

'No.' Charcoal tears sprang to Duchess Edita's eyes. 'They came in the night. They'd poisoned my guards and bribed my ladies-in-waiting. I'm not badly hurt, but they've thrown me in the dungeons and they . . . they say they're going to execute me!'

'No!' Bianca cried. 'I won't let them!'

Duchess Edita sucked in a deep breath. 'Bianca, I wish I could tell you to stay there, where you're safe. But the truth is, you can help me.'

'How? Anything!' Bianca gasped.

'Bring me the medallion,' Edita said. 'If I had it I could

–' She froze, and then the charcoal lines juddered into their original position, like a badly painted *animare* going back to the beginning of its cycle.

'Mother?' Bianca touched the paper gingerly, but it felt completely ordinary. 'Mother!' she shouted. The drawing stayed still. Her mother, the Duchess, was gone.

Chapter Sixteen

Bianca burst through the painted greenhouse into the Rose Gallery of the Duchess Catriona's palace and charged down the corridor towards her rooms. She shouldered past a group of courtiers, who gasped and clutched at their fans. She couldn't stop to think about what they thought of her, or where they thought she'd been for the last few days – she swore to herself if she could just sort out the Baron and Filpepi for good, she'd make explanations later. But first, she had to save her mother!

She banged through the door to her bedroom and pulled the bottom drawer from the chest so hard it slid right out and clattered onto the floor.

As soon as she looked into it she felt a horrible twisting in the pit of her stomach, as if she were standing on the parapet of the White Tower and looking down. Something was wrong. She couldn't put her finger on it . . . but something wasn't as she'd left it. Her heart pounding, she tugged out her apron and unrolled it.

The medallion wasn't in the pocket.

'No!' Bianca groaned. 'No, come on, come on . . .' She

pulled out everything from the drawer, unfolded the clothes, shook them, thrust her hands into the pockets so hard she split one of the seams. But there was nothing. The medallion was gone.

Someone had to have taken it. But who?

Who in La Luminosa hates me?

The answer was obvious. *Lucia.*

Bianca sprang to her feet, buoyed up on a wave of rage.

She was willing to bet Lucia had stolen the cathedral's painting, no matter what Cosimo said. Lucia had dedicated her life to making Bianca miserable. Of course she'd move on to taking Bianca's private things. Especially if she had any idea how much the medallion meant to Bianca. How much she missed di Lombardi and longed for a family of her own.

An image of her mother in a dank dungeon, facing death at the hands of the Baron, sprang to Bianca's mind and she sniffed back tears. She wouldn't let this happen. She'd get to the studio, and she'd make Lucia tell her where the medallion was.

She re-entered the passages through the painting in the Duchess's drawing room and ran all the way to Filpepi's study, but when she stormed down the stairs and into the studio the place was deserted. She stood in the doorway, breathing hard. Where were the apprentices? Had they all left? Was the studio shut down until the new master had been chosen?

Then Bianca slapped her forehead in frustration. Of course – the competition! It was happening *right now*.

Gasping in a deep breath, she ran back up the stairs, taking them two at a time, and sprinted through the passages to one of the paintings that hung in the Museum of Art. She threw open the door without even checking if anyone was on the other side. The room she stumbled into was empty, but she could hear the sounds of hushed, excited chattering echoing through the huge, high-ceilinged galleries.

Her breath rasped in her throat and her knees were shaky from running, but she followed the sound until she came into the central hall of the museum. A crowd had gathered and Bianca elbowed her way through to the front. A towering statue of Catriona's great-grandmother – the Grand Duchess Angelica – dominated the room, and at her feet three easels set up with paintings were being worked on by the three competitors.

On the left and right, two adult artists Bianca vaguely knew were hard at work. Laura Dexteris was painting a rather good portrait of Duchess Catriona, and the other one, a man who Bianca couldn't name, seemed to be trying to replicate one of di Lombardi's landscapes. But neither had any magic paints, and both looked worried as they glanced at the middle easel where Cosimo and Lucia were working together.

Their painting was truly stunning. They'd created a softly rolling landscape of green hills under a night sky bright with stars. On the closest hill, two trees grew, one silver and one gold. White flowers bloomed on the silver one, stirring in the breeze, and the golden tree's leaves shone out like a cool flame in the starlight.

Bianca was struck dumb for a second by its sheer beauty,

almost forgetting Lucia's treachery.

Wait a second – have they done all this with the magic paints I left behind?

No, there was no way there could have been enough. The painting was obviously heavily enchanted. There was light, movement, space . . . Bianca even thought she could hear a low heartbeat, calm and steady, measuring the time between each cycle of growth and death.

They've used a cuore. *That's not even a recipe I've used before!*

A gong sounded, and all four artists stepped away from their paintings. The two adults laid down their paintbrushes with sagging shoulders and shook their heads.

'It was a good effort,' said a lady beside Bianca, smoothing down the fur trim on her gloves. 'But who could beat the heirs to di Lombardi's secrets?'

'Looks like they've inherited his talent, too,' said the short man who stood next to her. 'Very promising.'

Duchess Catriona stepped forward and presented a signed and sealed contract to Cosimo and Lucia with a broad grin. The two new masters took the document with one hand each and bowed to the assembled crowd, who cheered and whooped. Bianca shrank back, her face flushing. She hoped she could get the medallion from Lucia, rescue her mother and return to La Luminosa without having to explain herself to the Duchess.

Catriona took a step back and the other apprentices broke from the crowd and ran over to Cosimo and Lucia, congratulating them with loud cheers. They all started to move off. Where were they going? Back to the studio? Bianca moved to follow them, determined not to lose sight of Lucia in the milling crowd.

'Bianca!' Duchess Catriona's shriek cut through the chatter and the applause like a hot knife through butter. Everyone in the room turned to look at the Duchess. Bianca briefly considered turning and running, but then the Duchess shouted again, 'Bianca, come here, *at once*!' and she couldn't make herself disobey. She tried to remember a little of her regal deportment lessons and not skulk or look ashamed as she walked over to where the Duchess was standing.

'Your Highness,' she said, curtseying low. 'Duchess Catriona, I'm sorry –'

'Oh, you'd *better* be sorry!' Duchess Catriona snapped. 'Where have you been? First you ignore your duties, and then just when you've promised me you'd fight for your position, you vanish! I thought you might have drowned, or been kidnapped! And now you come too late to compete . . . and don't even speak to me!' Catriona shook her head. 'How dare you curtsey to me as if you were just some servant – I thought you were my friend, Bianca, but it's been three days without a word! Tell me, where in the name of Saint Philip's beard have you *been*?'

Bianca trembled under Catriona's onslaught. Hot tears of guilt and shame stung her cheeks. The entire crowd, the entire *city*, seemed to be waiting for Bianca's answer. But how could she give an honest one with all these people listening?

And what was worse, the apprentices had already vanished, and the longer she stood here under Duchess

Catriona's iron gaze, the further she got from the medallion that could save her mother.

'I can't,' she said. 'I'm sorry.' She seized her skirt, turned and ran out of the room.

Sure enough, when Bianca got back to the studio the apprentices were gathered inside, drinking champagne from chipped mugs and laughing with Cosimo and Lucia. She threw open the door, and they all turned and stared at her.

'Bianca?'

'We've been worried sick!' yelped Rosa.

'We're sorry we were so horrible,' said Francesca. '*Aren't we*?' She elbowed Gabriella, who grunted vaguely and took another sip of champagne.

'Lucia, where is my medallion?' Bianca said simply.

'Your what?' Cosimo frowned. 'Bianca, if this is because of the competition . . .' He set down his mug of champagne. 'We all know you didn't actually *want* to be the master. Did you?'

Bianca shook her head. 'This isn't about that. I just want my medallion. Master di Lombardi left it to me in his will, and I left it in my room, and now it's gone.'

'Why do you think *I* took it?' Lucia said, her lip twisted with scorn. 'One of the maids probably stole it – and who can blame them? We all thought you'd run away! I suggest you run off back to the palace and –'

'Shut up, Lucia,' said a voice. Bianca blinked. It was Francesca. Her knuckles were white and her hands were trembling, making the champagne slop about in her mug,

167

but she met Bianca's eyes steadily. 'She's lying to you, Bianca. She did take the medallion – I saw her with it.'

Lucia snarled at Francesca. Bianca turned on Lucia – and so did Cosimo. He spoke before she could.

'Why would Francesca say that, Luce?'

Lucia's expression turned sour, but she sighed. 'Because . . . because I did take the stupid thing.'

'What?' Cosimo gaped at her. 'Luce, *why*? That was Bianca's personal property – you had no right! It wasn't even to do with the studio, not like –' He broke off.

'Not like the painting for the cathedral?' Bianca asked.

Cosimo's shoulders sagged. 'I'm sorry, Bianca. I was just so angry . . .'

Bianca shook her head. 'I don't care, Cosimo. Maybe you can make it up to me later. But right now, I *need* that medallion. Where did you hide the painting?'

Cosimo's face flushed and he walked over to one wall of the studio. Reaching behind a cabinet full of tools, he slid out the canvas, with its rolling hills and little group of pilgrims. The medallion was hanging from one corner. It fell and landed on the tiled floor with a damning clatter. Cosimo stared at it, and then looked at Lucia, hurt and confusion in his face. Bianca ran over and picked up the medallion, cradling it to her like a fragile creature.

'I've got to go,' she said.

'Where are you going now?' Cosimo said again.

But Bianca held up her hand. 'I can't explain.' She started to walk out, but stopped in the doorway and turned back to meet Cosimo's eyes . . . and Lucia's. 'Congratulations, that painting was . . . it was easily as good as one of Master di Lombardi's.'

She walked out, too anxious to feel anything but relief about finding the medallion. Now she had to save her mother.

Chapter Seventeen

Bianca hurried into the Piazza del Ferranti and saw Master Xavier's troupe still had their stage set up at one end, complete with the fateful tightrope strung between the roof and the tall pole. It was too early for them to be performing, but at least they hadn't moved, or left La Luminosa altogether.

She pushed through the curtain into the master blacksmith's shop. Only Olivia and another woman were there, dressed in their ordinary clothes. They were going through one of the trunks of props.

'Um, hello,' said Bianca. 'Is Marco here?'

'He's out back,' said Olivia, gesturing to a doorway beyond the furnace. 'Just through there.'

'Thank you!' Bianca hurried through the door and found herself in a little yard outside the blacksmith's shop. Marco was taking costumes out of a big bucket, wringing them out and hanging them up on a line strung across the yard. He looked up and dropped the tights he'd been holding back into the bucket.

'Bianca?'

Bianca grinned weakly at him. 'Hi,' she said.

'You came back,' said Marco. 'Is everything all right?'

Bianca tried not to actually sink to the floor with relief and gratitude. 'No!' she said. 'Something's gone terribly wrong. The Baron and Filpepi have attacked my mother and thrown her into her own dungeons. She told me to fetch the medallion to help her fight them off. Now I need the map to find my way back.'

Marco instantly ran over to one of the trunks and fished out the parchment.

At the sight of her best friend dropping everything to help her, Bianca felt like weeping. 'And I need you too; I can't do this by myself, please . . .' She gasped for breath.

Marco shrugged. 'You and me, defeating the Baron and Filpepi – it's just what we do, isn't it? It's like a hobby. I'll be back in time for the matinee.'

Bianca couldn't help but smile.

Marco unrolled the map and took in the maze of lines. 'We want to get back into the castle, right? I think if we run to the Chapel of Santa Pinta, that'll be quickest.'

'Thank you,' Bianca panted.

The Chapel of Santa Pinta was deserted, though the sound of slightly out-of-tune singing echoed around the stone arches.

'Must be having choir practice next door,' Marco whispered. 'Quick, let's get in the passages before they finish.'

Bianca winced as the singing abruptly broke off and a woman's voice started to berate the choir for their dull vowel colours. 'Doesn't sound like they'll be finishing any time soon!' she murmured.

The mural of Santa Pinta blessing the Duke di Angelo's horses was in the alcove right behind the altar. Bianca pulled out the paintbrush and muttered the magic words.

'Can I see the map?' she asked Marco. Marco handed it to her, taking the key and repeating the magic words as he turned it in the lock on the stable door. It swung inwards. Bianca unrolled the map a little way so she could find the chapel and trace the line that would get her back into the castle.

'I hope it's safe to come out in my drawing room,' she muttered. 'There could be another way, a bit closer to the dungeon. But it'll have to do.'

She handed the map back to Marco, and he reached out to take it.

Something glimmered on the back of his hand, and Bianca frowned. 'What's that you've got on you?'

Marco looked at his hand, and his cheeks darkened a bit. 'Oh, um . . . dunno,' he said.

'It's paint. And it's quite fresh.' Bianca grabbed Marco's hand and dragged her thumb over the splodge of shimmering silver paint. The edge flaked away, but the middle left a matching glow on Bianca's thumb. 'Have you been painting? But how did you get . . .' She looked up at him. 'Was it you? Did you help Cosimo and Lucia make the magic paint for the competition somehow?'

Marco didn't answer, just averted his gaze.

'Oh.' Bianca took a step back. 'You showed Cosimo and Lucia di Lombardi's notebooks? But they were in his secret workshop!'

172

Marco sighed. 'I went and got them, of course,' he said flatly. 'I was still inside the passages when I had the idea, so I went to the workshop and looked through all the books until I found the ones that had the magic recipes in.'

Bianca gaped at him. 'You stole them!'

Marco bristled. 'I did not! I just borrowed them. I only wanted to help. I was going to tell you – *if* you ever came back – I just forgot . . .'

But Bianca shook her head. 'Help? How is sharing my secrets with *Lucia* helping?' A horrible thought occurred to her. 'Marco! Did you tell her about my medallion? Did you help her steal that, too?'

'What? How could you say that?' Marco looked horrified.

'You didn't seem to have a problem taking other things from me!' Bianca snapped. 'It's *my* workshop now! Master di Lombardi left *me* the paintbrush, just like the medallion and the map. He knew I had important work to do, to find my mother and save Oscurita!'

'Yeah, but he didn't know he was going to die, did he? He thought he'd be around to teach you and Cosimo and the others all the recipes himself!'

Bianca gritted her teeth. 'Those were my secrets! You had no right –'

'No, Bianca, they were di Lombardi's secrets!' Marco folded his arms. 'I didn't know if you were ever coming back, and I knew he'd want his art to carry on!' Marco shook his head sadly. 'Part of me thinks you just liked being the only one who could do magic. But that's not fair. It's not good for anyone, not even you.'

The words stung Bianca – and they kept on stinging, like angry wasps swarming over a cup of sweet wine. 'You don't know anything.' She took another step backward, over the stable door threshold and into the passages. 'I don't want you with me. I don't need people I can't trust,' she said.

Marco's jaw dropped and he took a matching step back, into the chapel. 'Fine!' he said, and thrust the map at her. 'I was only trying to help while *Your Highness* was busy. Here, go and save your precious dark city by yourself!'

'I will!' Bianca snatched the map from his grasp and slammed the door before she could change her mind.

She stopped on the other side, her hand on the doorknob – but then she heard footsteps. Marco was walking away.

'*Fine*,' she hissed to herself. 'I will do this by myself.' She clutched the medallion so hard her knuckles stood out white against her skin. She had di Lombardi's gift. She'd free Edita, her mother would know how to use the medallion to defeat the Baron, and everything would be fine.

Bianca's drawing room was empty and dark when she pushed through the black and red painted door. The blue-tinged fire hadn't been set in the huge fireplace, and the only light came from the torches in the corridor and the soft, shifting glow of the *lux aurumque* flowers outside in the garden.

Bianca crept to the door and peered out into the passage.

There weren't any guards. Footsteps came towards her, so she pulled herself behind the arch of the door and held her breath.

A woman came into the passage. From her rough, plain

black dress and simple hairstyle Bianca guessed she was a maid. She was carrying a closed basket and humming a little tune. She passed Bianca's doorway and was gone.

Bianca frowned. The castle had been taken by the Baron – she'd expected a little bit more running and screaming. Some guards battling in the corridors, maybe some rooms on fire. Not maids humming little tunes and going about their day.

She felt silly as soon as she'd had the thought. When the Baron had taken over La Luminosa, he hadn't burned the palace down! He'd been subtle about it. Most of the people of La Luminosa hadn't even realised the throne was being stolen until it was all over.

I bet they've made a painted version of Mother and they're using her to keep everyone calm.

She had to get to the dungeon and find her real mother. Then they could expose whatever the Baron and Filpepi were doing.

If people were moving around the castle freely, perhaps she wouldn't even need to hide – but she would need a disguise. She ran into her bedroom and dug around in the cavernous wardrobes for the simplest clothes in Oscurita colours she could find. Pulling on a black coat over the top of her rough, paint-spattered dress, she wrapped a dark purple scarf loosely over her head and neck. She wasn't sure she'd pass for either a lady or a maid, but at least she wouldn't stand out like a dove in a rookery.

Grabbing a crystal jug of water that'd been left on the table, she emptied it into the garden, then walked out into the corridor clutching the empty jug.

Her disguise seemed to work – the few maids and courtiers she passed barely gave her a second glance. But the castle was eerily quiet. As she descended the back stairs and passed an archway that opened onto the courtyard, a clatter made her jump and pull her scarf over her face. But it was only a couple of guards moving armfuls of breastplates from the back of an armourer's cart into a pile by the barracks door.

Bianca abandoned her crystal jug before she started down the dimmer, twistier stairs that led to the dungeons.

She passed the alcove where she'd stolen the little bracelet, and reached into her pocket. The bracelet was still there. She ran her fingers over its smooth, cool surface. *I'm coming, Mother,* she thought. *I'm nearly there . . .*

More alcoves lined the stairs, each deep enough for a pedestal, a statue carved from black marble or a suit of gleaming silver armour. There were paintings on the walls too – stern portraits of people in suits of armour and dim craggy landscapes designed to inspire feelings of awe and despair at the same time.

She wondered if any of them had been painted by Master di Lombardi.

She almost walked right into the dungeons. The stairs rounded a corner and stopped, spitting distance from a guard sitting at a table, reading a book by the flickering light of a candle.

Bianca pulled back quickly and ducked into an alcove, slipping around the arm of a suit of armour and pressing herself into the darkness behind it, trying to catch her breath silently. She waited there, counting the seconds on her fingers until a full minute had passed, but there was no sound of a chair scraping back or footsteps approaching the stairs – the guard must not have seen her.

She edged out of the alcove enough to peer around the corner again. Her heart sank. She could see that beyond the guard there was another corridor, full of cells with iron bars for walls. Once she was in that corridor, she'd be out of sight of the guard and she could find her mother's cell – but there was no way to get there except to walk in front of the guard. However good his book was, she thought he'd probably notice a girl sneaking past him.

The candle-lit room where he sat, between the stairs and the cells, was barely two metres wide. She just needed to distract him for a moment and she could make it in a few steps.

But how could she draw him out without tipping him off to her hiding place?

Her hand slipped into her pocket again, looking for the soothing edge of the tiny bracelet. But her fingers found something else – something silky and fleshy.

She carefully drew out the slightly squished *lux aurumque* flower, shielding its light behind her coat. One of the petals had been crushed and the thick golden oil flowed out when she squeezed it. Her fingers tingled oddly under the power of the raw magic.

Her eyes fell on the painting that hung at the corner of the stairs, just opposite the turning. It was one of the portraits of people in armour – this one a pale woman, tall and strong-looking with short dirty-blonde hair and a seriously unimpressed expression. Bianca guessed she was a famous general, or maybe a wartime duchess. Her armour was slightly dented and the red and yellow banner that hung over her shoulder was bright but tattered.

The plan that started to form in Bianca's mind was horribly flawed. She had nothing to make paint with, only the raw, golden oil. And, she realised with a nasty jolt, she didn't even have a brush. Marco had pocketed di Lombardi's paintbrush key, and she'd driven him away . . . She wouldn't be able to open the doors to the secret passages again. Bianca dearly wished Marco was here now, even if he had given away her secrets.

Very, very carefully, without making a sound, Bianca edged back out of her hiding place. She kept herself out of the guard's line of sight as she crossed the stairs and sidled up to the painting. Then she picked the crushed petal from the *lux aurumque* flower and began to paint onto the canvas, using its petals like a paintbrush.

'*Lux aurumque, lux diffensis*,' she whispered, dabbing pools of oil onto the shiny places on the woman's armour. She reached out, her chest tightening as she reached over to sweep the magic substance onto the tattered tails of the banner. '*Animare volare*,' she breathed, sketching out a rough cycle of movement that she hoped would look at least a bit like the banner was flowing in the wind. Then she quickly took a step back towards her alcove.

As she watched, the banner began to flutter and the woman's armour gleamed as if the setting sun of La Luminosa was shining on her.

In fact, with the magic of the pure oil, the light grew brighter and brighter, and a slightly shimmering beam crept out from the painting, across the floor towards the weak, flickering light of the guard's room.

Bianca ducked back into the alcove and bit her lip.

Sure enough, there was a pause, an intake of breath, and then footsteps. Bianca edged forward, just a tiny bit, so she could see the guard as he approached the painting to stare at it, blinking in shock. He reached up with one hand to touch the fluttering banner, then hesitated, as if he thought it might bite him.

Bianca clenched her fists.

This is it. This is your chance. You have to go. Go!

She slipped out of the alcove, hugging the wall, got behind the guard, and then turned and hurried silently through the pool of candlelight and into the dark corridor behind.

Bianca pressed herself to the wall, out of the guard's line of sight.

Most of the cells were occupied. But the prisoners were silent and still. Many of them wore rags and had long, matted hair. A few lifted their heads to look at Bianca, but flinched away again at once.

Bianca edged along the corridor, peering into each cell. Were these people all the traitors her mother had talked about – the people who'd helped the pretender try to take her throne? Or were some of them her allies, imprisoned by the Baron?

She couldn't stop to figure it out now. Her heart pounded as she reached the final cell, right against the far wall. It was so dark she almost couldn't make out the hunched figure on the other side of the bars. But there was no mistaking the fine dress or the glitter of a silver bangle around the woman's wrist.

'Mother!' Bianca gasped.

The Duchess Edita was sitting in a bare cell, shivering with cold. Her hair, normally so elaborately arranged, hung limply over her face.

She looked up, saw Bianca and smiled. 'Oh my darling, you came!' she said, a little too loud for Bianca's liking. 'How wonderful!'

'Careful,' Bianca said. 'The guard . . .'

She turned to glance back down the line of cells, and something grabbed her from behind. She let out a yell, despite herself, and tried to wriggle away, but her arms were dragged together behind her back and tied so tightly her fingers immediately began to go numb.

A thunder-lamp crackled into life. Its blue-white light seemed almost blinding after the darkness. When Bianca's vision cleared, she found herself looking up into the sneering face of Piero Filpepi.

'Yes, how wonderful!' he said. 'It's my old apprentice. Still in need of discipline, I see.'

Bianca struggled hard against the ropes and tried to kick out, but Filpepi held her too tight. Another figure walked into her line of sight, pulling down the hood of a black cloak. Bianca was unsurprised to see it was the Baron da Russo, a smug smile spreading across his fat pink face. He reached towards her and Bianca writhed and tried to bite his hands, but it was no good. The Baron lifted the medallion from around her neck and held it up, gazing into its obsidian depths in wonder.

'Mother!' Bianca gasped. 'I'm so sorry! They tricked you!'

Duchess Edita stood, brushed down her dress and pulled her hair back into a neat bun.

'Filpepi, if you would,' she said calmly.

Bianca felt like the world had dropped out from under her and she was falling.

Filpepi fished a key from his pocket and opened the door to the Duchess's cell.

'What?' Bianca gasped.

Stepping out of the cell, Duchess Edita turned to look down at Bianca. Her dark eyes seemed like black holes in her face – without love or compassion, only a flicker of cruel amusement.

'I'm afraid, my darling, my dove, my sweetest . . . *I* tricked *you*.'

Chapter Eighteen

Duchess Edita made a clicking sound with her tongue and smoothed down her dress.

'This would have been much easier if you'd just brought the medallion with you when you first came. But no, you had to be *clever* about it.'

She held out a hand and the Baron dropped the medallion into it with a little bow. The Duchess draped it around her neck and ran her fingers over the obsidian surface.

Bianca opened her mouth to speak but shock prevented the words from escaping her throat. She looked up into her mother's face – its soft features a mirror of her own. But in her eyes Bianca saw only cruelty.

Edita smiled and turned to walk away.

'Move,' Filpepi said, and shoved Bianca forward. 'The Duchess wants you alive for the moment, but I'm just waiting for an excuse to be rid of you. So don't try to run, or you might find you tragically fall and impale yourself on my sword.'

'Traitor,' Bianca hissed. 'Duchess Catriona is going to have your head on a spike.'

'I'm no traitor,' said Filpepi. 'In fact, I am a patriot – a patriot of Oscurita.'

The guard stood to attention and saluted the Duchess as they passed. He didn't seem in the least surprised to see the Baron, Filpepi or Bianca.

Duchess Edita paused at the bottom of the stairs to look at the enchanted picture.

'Ah, still relying on Annunzio's obsession with pretty pictures? How amusing,' she said. 'Perhaps you will enjoy what comes next, after all.'

Anger and confusion brought tears to Bianca's eyes, blurring her vision. When she spoke her voice sounded like it was distant, spoken by someone else. 'Mother, I don't understand. Why are you doing this?'

But her mother didn't bother to answer. Bianca was marched in a daze to the top of the stairs. They started to pass other people – maids, guards and courtiers – but they averted their eyes and their faces were grim; not one of them seemed shocked to see their Duchess leading her own daughter through the Castle corridors with her hands bound.

They entered the throne room. Edita strode up to the raised platform where the throne of Oscurita sat. She ran her fingers over its silver back and black velvet cushions, and then turned to Bianca with a smile, as if waiting for her to speak.

But Bianca could only stand there shaking. The shock had subsided, leaving only raw pain and anger – anger at her mother for betraying her, and at herself for believing there was anyone in the world who really cared about her.

'You really have no idea what you've brought me, do you?' Edita said, still smiling.

Bianca stared hard at her mother, her lips pursed shut.

'Well?' Edita sat down on the throne, crossing her legs and holding up the medallion so it twirled and spun in the air. 'How clever you must have felt, discovering Oscurita as you did. The truth is, my dear, in the old days the people of the City of Light and the Dark City could come and go quite easily through the paintings.'

'But . . .' Bianca glanced at the paintings that hung on the walls around the throne room. They looked quite ordinary to her. 'But I've never heard of this place. Why doesn't anyone in La Luminosa know about it?'

Duchess Edita smiled. 'Oh, we kept to our own lands on the whole – few true Oscuritans could stand that nasty, unrelenting bright sun of theirs for long, and the stupid, clumsy La Luminosans were almost blind in this realm. They'd cause chaos more often than not, or stumble into the canals and drown!' The Duchess threw her head back and laughed at that hilarious idea. Bianca shuddered. 'But we had trade agreements, treaties, envoys. There was a La Luminosan embassy.'

'So what happened?' Bianca asked.

'The War of the Pretender . . . and Annunzio di Lombardi,' said Duchess Edita. A look of disgust crossed her face. 'He stole the power of the portals, and sank it all into this.' She held up the medallion. 'When he left Oscurita he used this to lock the city, to make sure nobody from Oscurita could travel to the City of Light. It even sucked the magic from his precious paintings, made them lifeless and dull.'

'But I thought Filpepi –'

'Oh yes, Oscuritan through and through,' said Edita. 'Annunzio didn't go to La Luminosa alone. He brought with him the two men who he knew could stand living in that horrible sunshine. A trusted friend and advisor – that would be Filpepi, here, his chief apprentice. Filpepi brought the Baron. Both of them were already under my command. They'd sworn to be my eyes and ears in the City of Light. And they remained loyal, all these years.'

The Baron swept a low bow, and Filpepi smiled slyly.

'I don't understand,' Bianca muttered, defeated. 'Why would you give me to di Lombardi, then? You're the Duchess! Why would you let him seal the paintings?'

Edita just stared at Bianca for a second. 'You haven't figured it out? Why would Annunzio have so much power and influence here? A simple painter? Why, you silly girl, do you think he cared for you as his own all these years?'

Bianca felt humiliated. She wished she knew the answers to the Duchess's taunting questions, but it seemed everyone around her had been keeping her in the dark her entire life. She stared at the floor, thinking of her old master. *I just thought he was wise and kind. He was Duchess Catriona's advisor; I never thought to wonder what he was to you . . .*

'I suppose I have taken some trouble to make sure that nobody in Oscurita ever uses his true title,' Edita admitted. '*Duke* Annunzio.'

Bianca's head snapped up.

'My father,' said Edita. 'Duke Annunzio Lombardi di

185

Oscurita was your grandfather.' She got up from the throne and started to pace in front of Bianca, twirling the medallion as she went. 'Duke Annunzio the Great, some used to call him. Annunzio the Artist.' Her face darkened. 'Annunzio the *Coward*. He loved the world of light more than he loved his own kingdom. His own daughter. He abandoned this city when it looked as if the war wouldn't go his way, and locked the doors behind him so nobody else could escape. Without the medallion I've been crippled, unable to truly cement my power.'

Bianca stared up at Edita as she paced back and forth.

None of this made sense. How could this bitter woman be the person who'd handed her over to di Lombardi and tearfully hugged him goodbye? There was no hint in the story di Lombardi had left Bianca that she'd been angry with him. But . . . could the painted story have been false? A pleasant lie to keep Bianca on his side?

She wouldn't believe that.

'Anyway,' sighed Edita, seizing the medallion in one hand and snapping the eight-sided obsidian pendant off its blue string. 'That's all over now. Finally, I'll be able to open all the portals with no need for paint. I will cross over into La Luminosa and take what's mine.'

'What's yours?' Bianca asked. 'But what is that?'

'Everything,' said Edita, looking at Bianca as if it was the stupidest question she'd ever heard. '*Obviously*.'

She knelt in front of the throne. Bianca spotted the octagonal hole in the throne-room floor and a chill shiver of inevitability crept over her as Edita slotted the medallion into it.

Eight beams of brilliant light and swirling shadow shot out from between the slabs in the stone floor, snaking across the room towards the walls. Bianca felt her jaw drop as all around her the murals and paintings started to glow and pulsate. Their colours ran and swirled, bleeding out into the air in thin streams, like a used paintbrush dropped into clear water.

'There, do you see?' Edita said, standing as the streams of colour threaded through the air around her. 'As quickly as paint dries on a canvas, the passages to the other world will be open once more!'

Bianca turned her face away, miserably, refusing to watch her wicked mother's triumph. She stared as a river of bright white and blue paint flowed out from a painting of a snowy landscape under a sky full of glittering stars. She turned every moment of the *storia* over and over in her mind as she watched the white stream cross the throne room, reflecting light onto the dark stones.

She'd seen Oscurita, then she'd seen it under attack. Her mother had run to the courtyard and given her over to di Lombardi – to Bianca's grandfather. It had all seemed so real! The paint had sparkled with colour and life as the tears had sprung to her mother's eyes . . .

Her mother's *blue* eyes.

Edita's eyes flashed in the reflected light from the swirling colours. They were a deep, dark brown.

'You are not my mother,' Bianca said.

Edita laughed. 'Dear God, I should hope not! My sister didn't deserve to rule. She had no ambition – and she was

187

just as much of a fool as you and my beloved father. Take her away,' she said, with a wave of her hand. 'But not to the dungeon. Take her to the Tower of Thorns.'

'Yes, Your Majesty,' said Filpepi with a bow. He dragged Bianca to her feet and pulled her away, ducking between the pulsating beams of colour that criss-crossed the throne room.

'You don't know Duchess Catriona!' Bianca yelled. 'Even if you get through, you'll never take La Luminosa!'

'A silly little girl, just like you,' Edita laughed. 'I don't think I'll have too much trouble!'

Bianca kept her eyes focused on her aunt's laughing face until the throne room doors slammed shut between them.

Chapter Nineteen

Two guards opened one of the doors at the top of the Tower of Thorns and threw her inside. Her knees were weak from the endless stairs, and as soon as the guards let go of her she dropped to the floor.

She felt an odd sensation on her numb hands, and then the ropes gave way. She turned to blink in surprise at the guard who'd cut the ropes, but he just shook his head.

'Much good may it do you,' he muttered. Then he slammed the door and turned the key in the heavy lock. Bianca heard him grumbling to his companion and the clanking of their armour as they started the long walk back down to the ground.

Bianca stumbled to her feet, rubbing her wrists, and looked around at her prison. It was bare, dusty, and freezing cold – but there was a bed, which even had a very old pillow and a blanket. Bianca seized the blanket and wrapped it around her shoulders. The sweat she'd worked up on the climb up the tower was quickly cooling on her neck and back, and the chill was so bad she thought it might actually turn to frost.

A needle-sharp blast of cold air hit her in the face and

she gasped. That was why it was so, so cold – there was no frame or glass in the window, just an empty hole in the thick stone wall. She went over to it and looked down, and then wished she hadn't. The window was easily big enough for her to climb out through, but it was a long, long way to the ground. The fall would kill her ten times over. When her heart had stopped pounding, she made herself look again, and realised why this was called the Tower of Thorns. Even if she did manage to use her scarf to lower herself carefully down and cling to the side of the tower, sharp-looking metal spikes stuck out of the tower at random intervals, like thorns on a rose stem. One slip and she'd be sliced to ribbons.

She shuddered and stepped back from the window, pacing the room trying to get warm. Her numb fingers clenched into white fists, as her body shook from frustration, as well as the cold: just when she believed she had everything she ever wanted – a home, a family – it had been taken away from her. An image of her aunt's cruel brown eyes flashed into her mind. *At least that wicked person isn't my mother.* It was a comforting thought.

Bracing herself against the icy wind she craned her neck, casting another look through the open window, surveying the black rooftops and canals of Oscurita, and the looming spires of its castle. Despite the shock, and behind her anger and humiliation, Bianca was relieved: her mother wasn't in league with Filpepi and the Duke. She could still be out there somewhere, hiding beneath one of those dark roofs.

She began pacing again, trying to form a plan of action. *So what are my options?*

After a few moments, she slumped down on the bed and stared into space.

I can sit here and rot while my evil aunt invades La Luminosa.

Or . . .

No, that's about it.

The idea of the unsuspecting Duchess Catriona facing an invasion from a land she didn't even know existed, with no time to prepare a defence, made Bianca feel sick with worry.

Bianca stood up. This was all her fault – but she wouldn't just sit here feeling sorry for herself, and she wouldn't cry. What would be the point, anyway? She was completely alone. She kicked out at the door and it gave a satisfyingly loud *BANG*.

'I think it's *locked*.'

Bianca jumped at the voice behind her. She spun round. 'Marco!'

Leaping to her feet, she sprang across the room, grabbing her friend and pulling him through the window. 'What? How?'

Marco was as white as an ice bear in a snowstorm. His arms and legs were shaking and sweat dripped from his hair as if he'd been out in the rain. He had thick layers of fabric wrapped around his hands and feet, but there was a cut across two of his fingers.

'How did you . . . ?' Bianca went over to the window and looked down. There were a few fluttering scraps of fabric caught on some of the sharp metal thorns. 'You did it! You got over your fear of heights!'

'I heard them say . . . you were imprisoned up here . . . so I climbed . . . oh god, s'cuse me,' he said, before bending over double, resting a forearm against the wall.

Bianca laughed, unable to quite believe Marco was right there before her.

'I had to come,' he said. 'Even if it meant climbing almost to the top of this *massive* tower. I couldn't leave you to do this by yourself. I had to come and tell you . . . you're a total idiot.'

'I know!' Bianca grinned.

'I mean it. You're a complete moron for not trusting me, because you don't know how sorry I am that I didn't tell you I was helping Cosimo. And you can't just stop being my friend because I won't let you.'

'Marco, I know! I'm so sorry!' She made a face. 'I'd hug you . . . only I'd be worried you might faint on me.'

'Fair enough,' Marco sniffed.

Bianca's heart sank. 'But I don't think I will be able to scale down there. I'm not an acrobat like you.'

'No problem,' Marco said, brandishing the paintbrush key. 'Turns out this key opens any lock in Oscurita.'

Bianca let out a yelp of joy and hugged Marco tight. She gave him another moment to recover, before moving towards the cell door: the key whined as it appeared to separate into tiny parts, shifting around and moulding to fit the lock as Bianca put it in. *Click*. She turned it. The door swung open.

'It worked! You were right.' Bianca shouted.

'Did you ever doubt me?'

'Of course not. Well . . . maybe for a second.' She grinned

again and they raced outside the door, the icy wind swirling down a winding stone stairway. Bianca could see doors to other cells leading off from the stairway below and, above, the stairs seemed to carry on up to another level.

Her blood froze in her veins. *Another level . . .*

'Marco! You said you climbed *almost* to the top of the tower?'

'Yeah . . .'

'Was there another level above my cell?'

'Yes . . . I think so. Actually, I think there were windows higher up the tower than yours. I guess there's a couple more cells up there. Why?'

She didn't wait to answer, charging up the stairway three at a time, then stopping in front of two thick wooden doors: one was swinging on its hinges, revealing a cold empty cell, but the other door was better kept and shut. Bianca heard Marco halt beside her.

'What's going on? Why have we come up here?'

Bianca's panting breaths came heavy and fast and her heart thundered in her chest. 'I think . . . I think . . .'

She raised a hand slowly, clutched the door's metal handle and pulled. Locked.

'H-hello?' said a voice. Bianca recoiled from the door and nearly tripped over her own feet.

'Is someone there?' said the voice. It was a woman's voice, soft and slightly raspy, as if she wasn't used to speaking at all. 'Please,' she said, more loudly, 'if you're there, say something!'

'I'm here,' said Bianca. She just caught the sound of an

intake of breath from the other side of the door.

'Oh! You sound so young. I could tell by your steps that you weren't a guard. It's been a long time since she's sent anyone up here with me.'

Bianca forced herself to stay calm. 'How long have you been a prisoner?' she asked.

'I . . . I'm not sure,' the woman admitted. 'Several years at least.'

Bianca couldn't imagine how awful it would be to be locked up for years. She had only managed two days under Lady Margherita's beady eye before escaping.

'Why are *you* up here? What did you do to aggravate Edita?' the woman asked.

'I . . .' Bianca began, but then her voice fell away.

The woman in the other cell let out a short laugh. 'Ha! Smart girl. You're probably wise to keep your own counsel. My sister has made Oscurita a dangerous place to trust anyone.'

'Your sister?' Bianca whispered, hope rising in her chest until she thought it might burst.

'Yes. My sister. The pretender to the throne who likes to call herself *Duchess* Edita. But she's no Duchess. Not while I'm alive.'

Bianca trembled as she spoke. 'Does she, um . . . does she have more than one sister?' she asked.

'Well – no,' said the woman. 'You must know that, though. I mean, you can't be so young you don't even know about the war!'

'You're her older sister? The rightful Duchess?' Bianca's

heart was beating so fast she thought Marco must have heard it, standing beside her.

'Don't let her hear you call me that, but yes,' said the woman.

'What is your name?' Bianca finally managed.

'I am Saralinda Zorna Lombardi di Oscurita. I am the rightful Duchess of Oscurita. But you can call me Saralinda,' she added.

'Saralinda,' Bianca whispered. 'Did you have a daughter?'

There was a long pause.

'Yes, I did,' said the voice. 'That's . . . that's also . . . *Everyone* in Oscurita knows that I sent my daughter away with my father when my sister took my throne.'

'Nearly thirteen years ago,' Bianca whispered.

'No . . . can it have been so long?'

Bianca drew in a deep, shaky breath. Perhaps this was all a trick. Perhaps it was a game Edita was playing.

But what if it wasn't?

'I grew up in La Luminosa,' she said. 'With an old man named Annunzio di Lombardi.' She heard Saralinda gasp. 'He told me that I was left on his doorstep. Nearly thirteen years ago. But I think . . . that's not what happened.'

'It can't be.' Saralinda's voice was half sob. 'Can it? My . . . my baby . . . Bianca . . .'

Bianca sensed her mother's body coming closer, pressing up to the other side of the door. She gasped, tears – just for once, tears of joy – spilling over her cheeks.

'If only we could see each other,' her mother said.

Bianca raised the magical key. It seemed like her whole

195

life had been leading up to this moment, to this doorway. 'We can.'

She grinned a huge, watery grin, and wrenched the key into the lock. She heard her mother step back with a gasp, as she practically threw herself at the heavy wooden door. It swung open.

Chapter Twenty

Her mother looked almost exactly like Edita. Her wrinkles were a little more pronounced and her eyes were blue, and her hair was messier and streaked with grey. Bianca could see that her cell was far more comfortable than her one – with a real bed and several layers of thick blankets and soft-looking pillows, as well as a chest of drawers and a mirror.

'Oh!' Saralinda gasped as she caught sight of Bianca. 'It is really you!'

Bianca nodded, frozen in the doorway, suddenly shy. But then Saralinda stepped forward and enveloped her in a hug. Bianca shut her eyes and tried to let the feeling wash over her. But it was hard not to remember the way Edita had put her arm around her and kissed her forehead, and how it had felt pretty much like the real thing . . .

Then Saralinda pulled away and wiped a tear from her cheek. She looked at Marco. 'And who is this?'

'This is Marco. My friend. My best friend in the world, *ever*!' Bianca amended, after a glare from Marco. 'He rescued me from my cell.'

Marco grinned shyly.

'Any friend of my daughter's is a friend of mine,' the Duchess said, smiling a wide, welcoming smile. She turned back to Bianca. 'This is . . . I can't believe you're really here! Oh, how did she find you? I sent you away so you'd be safe! Father closed the portals so that she couldn't get to you!'

'I came looking for you,' Bianca said.

'Where is your grandfather?'

Bianca swallowed. 'He died,' she said.

There was another pause, and a few short gasps of breath. Then her mother said, in a low, steady voice, 'Tell me what happened. Tell me everything.'

Bianca wished she could tell her mother everything she'd ever done, everything she'd ever heard or seen. Instead, she tried to keep her story short. Saralinda stayed quiet for most of it, but when Bianca mentioned di Lombardi's paintbrush key she gasped.

'That's how you got into Oscurita. And how you got into my cell?'

Bianca nodded before filling in the rest of the story: di Lombardi's will, the *storia*, the map, and the terrible mistake she'd made, assuming that Edita was her mother and believing that the Baron and Filpepi had imprisoned her in her own dungeon.

'I'm sorry,' she muttered. 'I was so stupid.'

'No!' said Saralinda. 'Believe me, Edita has tricked us all. But we have to get out of here. The Duke of La Luminosa has no idea she's coming, and if we don't warn him she'll run right over him.'

'The *Duchess* of La Luminosa,' Bianca corrected. 'The

Duke died a few years ago. His daughter Catriona's on the throne now.'

'Oh! Really?' Saralinda said. 'That's very sad. The Duke was a good man.'

'You knew him?'

'We met, once.'

'Well, his daughter is a great Duchess,' Bianca sighed. 'I can't believe I've done this to her. She's a good friend too.'

'All right,' Saralinda said, a look of steely resolve hardening her features. 'We have to get you back to La Luminosa before the portals finish opening.'

'We need a painting,' said Marco.

'We could try to make it back to the painting in my drawing room,' Bianca suggested. 'Or maybe I could open any painting in the castle?'

'There are guards on the tower, and the courtyard's swarming with soldiers,' Marco said. 'I don't think we'd get very far.'

'Well, we don't have any other options,' Bianca shrugged.

'You said Father trained you as his apprentice?' Saralinda said. 'Do you think you could paint your way back to La Luminosa?'

'Maybe.' Bianca's hand strayed into her pocket and she pulled out the *lux aurumque* flower. 'I . . . yes. I think so. But I'd need, well, paint!'

Saralinda smiled and turned to her desk. She moved aside some of the papers, and Bianca realised they weren't letters or documents – they were watercolour paintings. Saralinda held out a wooden tray subdivided into sixteen small sections, each holding a small piece of watercolour paint.

'Will this do?' she asked.

Bianca took a deep breath.

'I think it might!' She took the tray and turned to the wall. Saralinda brought her a small jug of water and Bianca swallowed, holding the paintbrush poised over the water. 'I've never made a magic painting from scratch,' she admitted. 'I've only converted ones that di Lombardi started. I don't know if there's something special he did . . .'

'Don't panic,' said Saralinda. She laid her hands on Bianca's shoulders and Bianca felt herself relax. 'Just do your best.'

Bianca took a deep breath, dipped her paintbrush into the water and then took a heavy brushful of paint. There wasn't much in the tray. Almost at once Bianca started to worry that she'd run out before she could even paint a picture of a door, let alone make it open. But she kept painting, sketching in the general shape and trying to pick the places that needed heavy colour with care so that she wouldn't use up all the precious paint . . .

'How come Edita lets you have all this stuff?' Marco asked Saralinda, behind Bianca.

'Being the rightful Duchess has its benefits, even in prison,' said Bianca's mother. 'Not all of Edita's guards are quite as loyal to her as she likes to think. Most of them are willing to hedge their bets by being kind to me, just in case I do take back the throne.'

Bianca washed the paint from her brush and took a step back.

'What do you think?' she asked.

'Oh! It's amazing,' said Saralinda.

'It looks really real!' Marco said. 'Let's get it open!'

'Yep,' said Bianca. 'That's the next step all right.'

'You're not sure how, are you?' asked Marco.

Bianca chewed her thumb. 'I . . . I have an idea. But if it doesn't work, I don't know what I'm going to do.'

'Well, we'll just have to fight our way out past the guards and the soldiers. With our amazing fighting powers,' said Marco. 'Or invent a pair of wings that'll let us jump out of the window and glide to the ground.'

'Heh.' Bianca smiled, feeling her heart lighten a bit. 'Actually, that doesn't sound like a terrible backup plan.'

'Oh yes, it does,' said Marco. 'I might have managed to climb up but I don't think I'm quite up to jumping down!'

'Well, then, you'd better pray this works,' Bianca said.

She pulled the *lux aurumque* flower out of her pocket and one by one picked the last remaining petals from it and crushed them between her fingertips, squeezing their magical golden oil into the jug of water. By the time she'd finished it was glowing and swirling in the jug. She held the jug close to her face and closed her eyes.

'All right. Let's see.' She tried to dig deep inside herself, to find the right magic words, and the words seemed to well up inside her. '*Lux aurumque* . . . please open the way,' she whispered. '*Dolce casa, bella casa.* Bring us home.'

She dipped her brush into the mixture and paused, the brush held in the air, for a second. Then she began to paint, and where she painted, the door solidified. The handle popped out of the wall and the hinges dug in. All the way around the edge of the door, a gap opened up, as if there really was something behind it. Finally, Bianca filled in the dark recesses of the lock, and her paintbrush vanished several centimetres into the wall.

She turned the brush around and fitted the key end into the lock. It turned, and the door swung open. Bianca let out a happy, exhausted groan at the sight of the familiar paint-speckled passages on the other side.

She'd done it. She'd made her own doorway from scratch.

'Let's go!' She stepped through, and Marco followed her. But when Bianca turned back, she realised her mother wasn't following. 'Mother?' she asked, walking back into the cell.

Saralinda smiled and clasped her hands over her chest. 'Oh, Bianca! You really have inherited your grandfather's talent. Far more than I ever did! I'm so glad.' She hugged Bianca again.

Grandfather, Bianca thought. *Am I really the great Annunzio di Lombardi's granddaughter?* She felt as if she might burst with pride.

Then Saralinda pulled away. 'And now you two must get going.'

'But you have to come! I can't leave you here with Edita.'

'Oh don't worry about me,' said Saralinda. 'I have to stay in Oscurita. The Resistance will be waiting for me to contact them – and I can't live in La Luminosa. It's just like Marco here and Oscurita. Some of us just can't cope with the light – or the darkness. Not even . . . not even for love,' she added softly, reaching out a hand and tenderly tucking a strand of hair behind Bianca's ear.

Bianca's heart skipped a beat. 'Do you . . . mean my father?' she asked. 'Was he from La Luminosa?'

'He was,' said Saralinda. 'But there's no time for this – you must go, and warn the young Duchess that Edita is coming. We'll see each other again soon, I promise, and I'll tell you all about him. For now, know that he was a wonderful man, a hero, and he would have loved you dearly. Now go on! We'll meet again.'

Bianca stepped back into the passages, and she and Marco waved to Saralinda. Then Saralinda slowly closed the painted door, leaving them alone.

Marco looked at Bianca. 'Are you OK? That was a bit intense.'

Bianca sucked in a long breath. 'I . . . have got a city to save!' she said firmly. 'Come on!'

Chapter Twenty-one

Bianca and Marco sprinted along the passageways, glancing at the doors they passed. Bianca gritted her teeth in frustration. They could get back into La Luminosa through any one of them, but it wouldn't do them any good to run out into a random city square or someone's house and start shouting about an invasion – they had to get to the palace and warn the Duchess.

'Hey, Bianca,' Marco panted.

'What?' Bianca asked.

'It worked!' He grinned at her as they swung around a corner. 'You painted a magic door! How does it feel to be the true heir of Master di Lombardi?'

'It'd feel a lot better if my crazy aunt wasn't mustering an invasion force right now,' Bianca said, but she grinned back.

Suddenly Bianca skidded to a halt, staring at one of the doors.

'Marco!' she yelled after him.

Marco doubled back, panting. 'What?'

'This is a painting that's in Filpepi's house! We can get the other apprentices to help us!' She threw open the door and jumped out without looking to see if Marco was following. She landed with a thud on the black-and-white tiled floor in Filpepi's hall.

She picked herself up and glanced around at the paintings that lined the walls.

'They seem normal,' she gasped.

Marco climbed out of the painting, shutting the door behind him. 'No sign of pulsating,' he said. Bianca glanced up at him. 'I saw it when I was sneaking into the castle. The paintings all looked like they were bleeding.' He shuddered. 'Too weird.'

'Maybe we still have some time.' Bianca wrung her hands, half nervous and half praying. 'We have to find the others.'

Marco held up his hand. 'Hear that?'

'. . . *still say . . . shouldn't have let her go . . .*'

The sound of squabbling – wonderful, ordinary apprentice squabbling – was coming from the studio. Bianca ran over to the doors and threw them open. The apprentices were all there, either painting, sculpting or sketching – though Rosa was standing with her arms crossed, eyeballing Cosimo and Lucia. She looked up as Bianca burst through the doors.

'Bianca! We're so glad you came back,' she said. 'Aren't we?'

'Of course we are,' Cosimo said, with a slightly pointed glance at Lucia.

'Yes,' Lucia sighed. 'Of course.'

'Thank you,' said Bianca. 'But there's something very important I have to tell you, and you have to believe me, because I don't have time to argue about it.'

'What on earth are you wearing?' Gabriella sneered. 'You look like a nun.'

Bianca's hands strayed to the pockets of her black coat and the purple scarf that was still wrapped loosely around her head.

Then she straightened her back and gave Gabriella a small smile. *I look like an Oscuritan princess*, she thought. She explained about Oscurita and Edita and Saralinda and the medallion as quickly as she could.

'Someone call a doctor,' agreed Gabriella. 'She's actually gone completely mental. Being our master's not good enough, now she's a princess as well!'

But Lucia's jaw had dropped and her skin had turned slightly yellow. 'Duchess Edita? Oscurita?' she said weakly. All the apprentices turned to her and she swallowed. 'I . . . I used to work late sometimes, when Filpepi was still in charge. I used to hear him talking to the Baron. They often mentioned Duchess Edita. Sometimes he said . . . he missed Oscurita. I just assumed they were talking in code or something.'

There was a shocked silence as this sank in.

'Edita is real,' Bianca said. 'And she's coming. *Now*.'

'But . . . an *invasion*?' Sebastiano gasped. 'We haven't been at war for a hundred years! What are we going to do?'

Domenico side-stepped over to him and their hands snaked together. 'How can we help?'

'We have to tell the Duchess,' said Cosimo. 'If this is really happening, we've got to raise the alarm.'

'Marco, can you stay here and find those notebooks?'

206

Bianca asked. 'There might be something else in them that can help us. Some kind of . . . I don't know. Defensive magic, or a trick we could use.'

'I'll help,' said Lucia. 'I've been working on the notebooks since Marco brought them to us.'

Bianca took a deep breath and swallowed her desire to tell her not to touch her grandfather's notebooks. She nodded. 'Good. Get everybody making anything that looks useful, and we'll go to the palace.'

'Maybe some of di Lombardi's inventions would help,' Marco suggested. He met Bianca's eyes and raised an eyebrow.

'Good idea,' said Cosimo. 'Sebastiano, Domenico, run back to di Lombardi's house and search it for anything useful we might have left behind. Now we need to get going,' he said, running over to Bianca and patting her on the shoulder. 'If we're going to get to the palace on foot before this invasion begins –'

'Wait!' Bianca said. She took the paintbrush key from her pocket and held it up.

'What's that?' Rosa asked. 'Is it a paintbrush? Or a key?'

Bianca walked over to the closest painting with a door – a painting of the grand ballroom in the palace. She climbed up into it and stood at the edge of the magical space, the animated figures waltzing and spinning behind her.

'I wanted to keep this for myself. But that was really selfish of me.' She met Marco's eyes and then looked away again. 'I just wanted to be special. Well, I was Mistress Bianca briefly, and that was pretty horrible, and apparently now I'm a princess, and that hasn't been a bundle of laughs either. I think maybe "special" is overrated.'

'Bianca, what are you saying?' Rosa asked gently.

Bianca shook herself. 'I'm saying . . . this.' She turned and put the key into the door at the side of the painting and it swung open.

The apprentices gathered around the painting, gazing in wonder at the torchlit passageway beyond.

'These passages link all of Master di Lombardi's paintings, all over the city. We can get to the palace quicker this way.' She reached out and Cosimo took her hand to let her help him up into the painting. Bianca held the door open and then turned, caught Domenico's eye and tossed the paintbrush key to him. His jaw dropped, but he caught it and held it gingerly, as if it might bite him. 'Marco, take Domenico and Sebastiano to Master di Lombardi's secret workshop,' she said.

'Will do, Your Highness,' said Marco, and winked at Bianca.

Bianca smiled at the other apprentices as they gaped at her. 'I'm glad I've told you all. This is too important for secrets – we have to work together to save La Luminosa!'

'Oh!' Duchess Catriona slapped the arms of the throne and jumped to her feet in a very unladylike manner. 'Bianca, what are you doing now?'

Everyone in the throne room gaped in surprise as Bianca and Cosimo climbed out through an open door in one of the paintings on the wall.

'I swear by my crown, Bianca,' Catriona yelled, her face so red her freckles completely vanished. 'If you don't explain yourself *right now* I shall tell Captain Raphaeli to get out the head spikes. You know he'll obey me!'

Bianca glanced at Captain Raphaeli, standing by the side of the throne, and caught his shoulders sagging in a long-suffering sigh.

'Duchess.' Cosimo led Bianca through the crowd of courtiers and gave Catriona a low bow as they approached the throne. 'I'm sorry to burst in on you like this. But Bianca has a very good reason for the way she's been behaving recently.'

Oh thanks, Bianca thought – but it seemed to have worked on Catriona. She plonked herself back on the throne in a ballooning rustle of silk.

'I'm listening. This had better be very, very good.'

Bianca launched into her tale. Catriona deserved the fullest version of the story but there wasn't time. When she came to the point where she had to claim to be royalty, the daughter of the rightful Duchess of Oscurita, there were titters of dismissive laughter from the crowd. Bianca saw Captain Raphaeli's fist clench on the hilt of his sword.

But Duchess Catriona listened seriously and calmly as Bianca finished her story, and then got majestically to her feet.

'Bianca, I know you would never lie to me,' she said, raising her voice so that everyone in the throne room would hear her. 'But an invasion, Bianca? Are you sure?'

Bianca opened her mouth to speak, but then one of the

courtiers let out a shriek. 'The paintings!' he gasped. 'Look at the paintings!'

Bianca turned, though she knew exactly what she'd see. The colours were glowing and pulsating, as if each painting had a heart pounding behind its canvas. Streams of translucent reds and greens and blues and whites and golds pumped from the surface of each picture with every heartbeat.

'It's happening,' she said.

Duchess Catriona stepped close to Bianca and spoke, lowering her voice so that only Bianca could hear. 'Well, Lady Bianca! So you are following in your grandfather's footsteps after all. My royal artist . . . and loyal defender and spy.'

'I'll always be your defender, Your Highness,' Bianca said.

Duchess Catriona squeezed her hand and then raised her voice so that it filled the throne room. Bianca could almost imagine it ringing from the rooftops of La Luminosa.

'Captain Raphaeli, call your forces together. We must prepare for war.'

Bianca raised her head and squared her shoulders. She was ready to fight. Oscurita was in her blood, but La Luminosa was her home too, and she wasn't going to let Edita take either one from her.

I'll save them both.

I'm ready.

Read on for an exclusive extract from the next
book in The Last Apprentice series:

THE PAINTED WAR

THE PAINTED WAR

The museum doors splintered. The Oscuritan army was breaking through! In moments they would break out of the museum and invade the streets of La Luminosa.

The forces of La Luminosa visibly recoiled, all of the volunteers and several of the soldiers taking half a step back.

'Stand your ground!' Captain Raphaeli shouted, turning his horse and drawing his sword. 'Defend your homes!'

Bianca jumped down from the fountain and sprinted through the crowd to the front line.

'Captain!' she shouted. 'Captain Raphaeli!'

Raphaeli looked down, and his face drained of colour for a moment. 'Bianca! Lady Bianca, what are you doing? This is a battlefield, you can't be here!'

Bianca ran up to him and grabbed the reins of his horse. She looked up at him, and then spoke quickly and quietly. 'I . . . I'm so sorry. I couldn't find the Duchess. My mother hadn't heard anything about her being brought to Oscurita. She said she's probably being hidden in La Luminosa. And then . . . then . . .' She couldn't do it. 'I don't know how to find her. I'm so sorry.'

213

'None of this is your fault,' Raphaeli said. 'You know that, don't you? It's because of you that we even have this number of fighters. If you hadn't warned us when the passages first reopened, we'd be overwhelmed.' He shook his head. 'If only we'd had more time to train some of these volunteers. They don't know how to follow orders; they'll just listen to whoever shouts loudest.'

'It should be the Duchess leading them into battle,' said Bianca.

'I wish I could disagree.' Captain Raphaeli's horse danced a few steps away as the Oscuritans bashed into the museum doors again. Raphaeli didn't blink. 'I hate the idea of her fighting in battle, but she'd be worth twenty soldiers if she was here. I had some people climb up to the high windows on the museum and look inside. Edita's in there on a black charger, and her people are clearly rallied around her.'

'Is it . . . is it hopeless?' Bianca asked.

'No!' Captain Raphaeli said firmly. 'But I'd give my right arm for a hundred more soldiers,' he added. 'Or for Duchess Catriona to be here. Filpepi's painted doll would do! The people need to see what they're fighting for.'

An idea hit Bianca so hard she almost rocked back on her heels from the force of it. 'Filpepi's painted Duchess . . .' she breathed. She looked up at the Captain and forced a smile. 'I think I have a plan,' she said. 'I have to go.'

'Be careful, Bianca!' Captain Raphaeli called after her as she turned and ran off. 'Keep away from the fighting!'

Bianca hurried out of the crowd and out of the piazza, pausing as she passed the young guard who was still giving orders to new arrivals. She caught her breath and stared up at the stars, trying to think her plan through.

It was all very well to know that it was *possible* to magically create soldiers out of paint. But she had to be practical. The best supply of paint and tools was, by far, di Lombardi's secret workshop. But how could she get there? All the paintings were in the museum, and even if she could get into the passages, they would be swarming with Oscuritan soldiers.

'Bianca!' That was Marco's voice. Bianca looked around, unable to see him at first, until suddenly the crowd parted and she spotted him waving at her. She ran over.

He was standing with his father, Master Xavier, who was carrying his big wooden staff with the round orb on the end. Bianca had never quite noticed how heavy it looked before, or how easily it could be used as a club. Most of the rest of the troupe were there too – Olivia was wearing silver-painted wooden costume armour and carrying a prop scimitar that'd been sharpened until its edge glinted, and Bianca saw the fire twins Carmina and Valentino and half a dozen others wielding weapons that looked like they'd been cobbled together from props and bits of staging.

'Bianca, there you are,' said Cosimo. Bianca turned to see him standing beside the tumblers. Behind him, Lucia, Ezio, Gennaro and Rosa stood. They were rather worryingly well armed with palette knives, hammers, chisels and shears.

'Where are the other apprentices? Are they safe?'

'They've gone to the island,' Lucia said. 'And that's where you need to go too!'

'I agree,' said Master Xavier. He looked down at Marco with a mixture of pride and abject terror. 'And please take my son with you – by force, if necessary.'

'I told you,' Marco said firmly, 'I can't go. I have to help protect the city!'

'Actually, I do want Marco,' Bianca said. 'Marco, where's the underwater craft?'

'Still moored up by the Bridge of the Cats, as long as someone hasn't run off with it,' said Marco.

'Can we use it to get into the secret workshop?'

Marco's face lit up. 'Yes! We can go in through the trap door into the canal!'

'We need to go, right now.'

Master Xavier's face was a picture of relief, and he and Olivia gathered Marco into a tight three-way hug. Bianca ran forward and gave each of the apprentices a huge hug in turn – even Lucia, although she saved her hardest squeeze for Rosa.

'Good luck,' she said. 'It's going to be OK.'

She grabbed Marco's hand and dragged him back down the street towards the Bridge of Cats.

'What are you going to do?' Marco asked, running towards the craft.

'Something that's never been done before,' she shouted after him. 'It might be dangerous. I . . . have no idea if I can undo it.'

'Do you think it might help?' Marco asked.

'I hope so.' Bianca didn't know. But she had to try, for the sake of her beloved city and everyone in it.

Imogen Rossi

Imogen Rossi grew up in London but her favourite place in the world is Venice during the Carnival. She spent most of her summer holidays in Italy, where she passed the time doodling and writing stories. She loves to paint, though she isn't very good at it, and she sings in a choir. She most enjoys stories involving mystery, magic and time travel. She has a collection of Venetian carnival masks and two cats named Leonardo and Michelangelo (Lenny and Mike for short).